P

C. S. Forester was born

stationed as a governmen

Hospital, and after leaving Guy's without a degree he turned to writing as a career. His first success was *Payment Deferred*, a novel written at the age of twenty-four and later dramatized and filmed with Charles Laughton in the leading role. In 1932 Forester was offered a Hollywood contract, and from then until 1939 he spent thirteen weeks of every year in America. On the outbreak of war he entered the Ministry of Information and later he sailed with the Royal Navy to collect material for *The Ship*. He then made a voyage to the Bering Sea to gather material for a similar book on the United States Navy, and it was during this trip that he was stricken with arteriosclerosis, a disease which left him crippled. However, he continued to write and in the Hornblower novels created the most renowned sailor in twentieth-century fiction. He died in 1966.

The Ship

[illegible] where his father was [illegible] he studied medicine at [illegible]

[illegible]

The Ship

C. S. FORESTER

PENGUIN BOOKS

PENGUIN BOOKS

Published by the Penguin Group
Penguin Books Ltd, 80 Strand, London WC2R 0RL, England
Penguin Group (USA) Inc., 375 Hudson Street, New York, New York 10014, USA
Penguin Group (Canada), 90 Eglinton Avenue East, Suite 700,
Toronto, Ontario, Canada M4P 2Y3
(a division of Pearson Penguin Canada Inc.)
Penguin Ireland, 25 St Stephen's Green, Dublin 2, Ireland
(a division of Penguin Books Ltd)
Penguin Group (Australia), 250 Camberwell Road, Camberwell, Victoria 3124, Australia
(a division of Pearson Australia Group Pty Ltd)
Penguin Books India Pvt Ltd, 11 Community Centre,
Panchsheel Park, New Delhi – 110 017, India
Penguin Group (NZ), cnr Airborne and Rosedale Roads, Albany,
Auckland 1310, New Zealand
(a division of Pearson New Zealand Ltd)
Penguin Books (South Africa) (Pty) Ltd, 24 Sturdee Avenue,
Rosebank, Johannesburg 2196, South Africa

Penguin Books Ltd, Registered Offices: 80 Strand, London WC2R 0RL, England

www.penguin.com

First published 1943
Published in Penguin Books 1949
This edition published 2006
1

Set in 11/13pt Monotype Dante
by Palimpsest Book Production Limited, Polmont, Stirlingshire
Printed in England by Clays Ltd, St Ives plc

ISBN-13: 978-0-141-02937-5
ISBN-10: 0-141-02937-4

Dedicated
with the deepest respect to the
Officers and Ship's Company of
HMS Penelope

With half a million men in the Royal Navy at the time this story was written, it is inevitable that there should be some coincidence of names and ranks between characters in this book and officers and ratings now serving. This is so inevitable that the author has made no attempt to avoid any such coincidence; all he can do is to assure the reader that he has attempted neither portrait nor caricature of any living person.

I

From the Captain's Report

. . . and at 11.30 the attacks ceased, although enemy aircraft were still occasionally visible . . .

Paymaster Commander George Brown put his fountain pen back into his pocket, put on his cap and got up from the table where he had been ciphering.

'I'm going for a prowl,' he told the petty officer beside him.

He slid his rather rotund bulk out through the narrow door and down three successive ladders, turning each corner and making each steep descent with the careless facility of long practice, even in the darkness that prevailed with the doors all shut. Emerging on the deck he stood and blinked for a moment in the sunshine, clear, sparkling sunshine which gave less warmth than might be expected in the Mediterranean in March. The sky was blue and the tossing sea was grey, the two colours blending exquisitely, the white caps and the white stretch of the wake completing the colour scheme to an artist's satisfaction.

The Paymaster Commander took a step or two farther into the waist, and stood and blinked again. He was not wasting time, nor idly taking the air; he was, as he might have expressed it himself, engaged in out-thinking

Mussolini. The guns' crews at the four-inch guns, at the pompoms and at the '50 calibre machine guns were standing at their stations; as *Artemis* rolled in the heavy sea the brass cases of the ammunition expended in beating off the last attack jangled on the iron decks on which they lay heaped like autumn leaves.

The men at the guns were vigilant and yet relaxed, they would lose no time, not one-tenth of a second, in opening fire should another attack be launched, but they were not wasting their strength in staying keyed up unnecessarily. These men were veterans of nearly three years of war, three years during which at any moment death might swoop at them from the skies, and every movement they made showed it. The weapons they handled were part of their lives by now; not toys for formal parade, nor wearisome nuisances to be kept cleaned and polished in accordance with a meaningless convention; those cannons were of the very essence of life, as was the long rifle to the frontier pioneer, the brush to the artist, the bow to the violinist. In a world where the law was 'kill or be killed' they were determined to be the killers and not the killed – the tiger stalking his prey lived under the same law.

The Paymaster Commander had finished out-guessing Mussolini; his experience of aerial attacks told him that another was unlikely in the immediate future. And at the same time what he knew from the signals he had been deciphering made him quite certain that the respite was only a respite, and that more desperate work lay ahead even than beating off Italian dive bombers. He turned into the galley, where the Chief Petty Officer Cook, burly and competent, stood waiting for orders – the only man in the ship (until the Paymaster Commander decided to take his stroll), apparently, not engaged in the business of making the ship the complete fighting machine; and yet he, too, had his part to play.

'Half an hour to send food round,' said the Paymaster Commander. He picked up the telephone. 'Wardroom.'

In the wardroom the telephone squealed plaintively and the Surgeon Lieutenant Commander answered it.

'Wardroom.'

'Hullo, PMO Purser here. Let's have some of my boys back. You can spare 'em.'

The Surgeon Lieutenant Commander looked round him. When HMS *Artemis* was at action stations the wardroom ceased to be the officers' mess and became the Medical Distributing Station. Here the wounded were brought for treatment – the sick bay, forward under the bridge, was both too small and too exposed to be used as anything other than a dressing station. The two casualties were quiet now, and the stretcher-bearer force was squatting on the deck. The Surgeon Lieutenant Commander carried grave responsibility in yielding to the Paymaster Commander's request. A sudden attack might leave twenty – fifty – wounded on the decks; a score of lives might depend on prompt collection and treatment. Wounded left lying were bad for discipline, bad for morale, apart from the guilty conscience which would torment the Surgeon Lieutenant Commander if his job were not properly done. But he had been shipmates for two years with the Paymaster Commander, and could appreciate his cool judgement and sober common sense. Pay was not the kind of man who would make a frivolous or unnecessary or ill-timed request. He could trust him.

'Right-o, Pay. I'll send 'em along.'

He looked along the row of squatting forms.

'You eight. You're all galley party? Report to the Paymaster Commander at the galley.'

The eight queerly dressed men – between them all they hardly bore a single trace of uniform clothing – scrambled to their feet, and doubled forward into the sunshine which illuminated the waist and halted at the galley. The Surgeon Lieutenant Commander watched them go. Perhaps it was the sight of the ragged group running which started a train of subconscious memory, starting with the recollection of an inter-hospital cross-country race; the Surgeon Lieutenant Commander suddenly found before his mind's eye a picture of the interior courtyard at Guy's – the green grass, the dribbling fountain where pigeons tried to wash off London grime, the nurses, white aproned, in blue or lilac uniforms, first year students carrying microscopes, third year men lounging, pipe in mouth and comically manly, out from the gloomy entrance to the dissecting-room, the youthfulness and eager anticipation of the best in life. All bombed to hell now, he had heard. The Surgeon Lieutenant Commander shook the vision from him as though it were water out of his eyes when he was swimming; he turned back to take a fresh look at the rating with the head wound. There was a chance that the wounded man might live and be none the worse for his experience.

In the galley the Paymaster Commander was ready with the scheme he had long mapped out, had tested in a dozen engagements. He had six hundred men to feed, and none of them had eaten for six hours. The Paymaster Commander thought of the hungry six hundred with a queer tenderness. He was a man born for parenthood, for self-sacrifice, to think for others. If Fate had made him a millionaire, he might have been a notable philanthropist; if Fate had given him children, he might have been the much loved father of a family, but Fate had ruled that he should be a childless man and a poor one. And as the senior officer of the paymaster branch in a light cruiser his inborn instincts had play in other directions. At present his thoughts were queerly paralleling those of the housewife planning what would be best for her menfolk getting in the harvest or working at the mill – it was only common sense that they should be given the best available, and it was pleasant that that should be what he liked doing anyway.

There was no flame in the range by which cooking could be done – the oil fuel for the range had all been safely drained away below where it was less likely to start a fire – but there was a steam jet, and superheated steam, not the flabby vapour that issues from a kettle's spout, but steam at four hundred degrees, live, active steam, can do remarkable things in the quickest time. The cook was already putting the ingredients into the cauldron. No economy soup this, but the best the ship could provide, the best the limited imagination of the Admiralty could encompass for the men who fought the battles. To make the forty gallons of soup necessary the cook was ripping open four dozen vast tins of tomatoes; stacked round him were the sixteen tins of corned beef which would go in next. The Paymaster Commander, without wasting time, took the fourteen pounds of cornflour and began to mix it into a paste with water so as to make it smooth for admixture with the soup. While he was doing so he issued his instructions to the men who came panting up to the galley at the Surgeon Lieutenant Commander's orders.

'Get going on those sandwiches,' he said. 'Hopkins, open the tins. Clarke and Stanton, cut the meat. The rest of you see to the spreading.'

The men fell naturally into the parts they had to play, like actors in a well-rehearsed performance. The long loaves which the cook's crew had made and baked during the night were run through the slicer, the slabs of corned beef were slapped on the buttered slices, and the completed sandwiches were stacked aside; the knives flickered with the speed at which they worked, and they had no time for speech except for brief sentences – 'Let's have another tin here, Nobby'; 'More butter here!'

Cornflour, meat, vegetables, all had gone into the soup cauldron, and now the Chief Petty Officer Cook dropped in the three pounds of sugar and the handfuls of herbs which were his own contribution to the formula for producing appetizing soup. He stirred with his vast ladle, and then moved the lever of the steam valve round its pipe. Only a slight crackling and tremor indicated that steam from the ship's boilers – steam as hot as red-hot iron – was heating up the cauldron.

The Canteen Manager and his assistant came to attention before the Paymaster Commander.

'We've been sent to report to you from the wardroom, sir,' said the Canteen Manager.

'Very good. Start on the cocoa. Murchie, get those pickles opened.'

The Paymaster Commander swept his gaze round the galley. The soup was nearly hot, the forty gallons of cocoa were preparing, the mass of sandwiches nearly completed. He checked the other tubs – they were full of fresh water, in accordance with his standing orders. The Paymaster Commander had fought in another battle, once, in a cruiser which had filled with water nearly to the level of her maindeck. Desperate determination and brilliant seamanship had brought her in tow back to harbour after forty-eight hours of struggle against wind and sea, submarines and aircraft; but those forty-eight hours had been spent without drinking water, thanks to the holing of some tanks and the submersion of the others. The Paymaster Commander remembered the insanity of thirst and fatigue, and never again would he allow his men to suffer that agony as far as it was in his power to mitigate it. These tubs held half a gallon for each man of the ship's company – men could go for days on two pints of water if necessary.

His final inspection completed, the Paymaster Commander stepped out again on deck, balancing against the roll and heave of the sea. The horizon was still clear; there were no planes in the sky. On the port quarter the convoy still rolled along over the grey surface. Mussolini, the Paymaster Commander decided, was not going to cause any more trouble immediately; so he took up the telephone again and said 'Commander'. The Commander answered from his Damage Control Station on the boat deck.

'Pay here, Commander. Dinner's ready to serve. May I pipe to that effect?'

'Yes, carry on,' said the Commander.

The Paymaster Commander made his way forward and heaved himself up over the prodigiously high coaming to the foot of the ladder leading to the bridge.

'Bosun's mate,' he ordered, 'pipe "cooks to the galley".'

The Bosun's mate switched on the loudspeaker, and the eerie squeal of his pipe went echoing through every corner of the ship.

He was a north-country man, and his years in the Navy had not eliminated the north-country tang of his speech. He drew out the double O of the word 'cooks' until it was a treble or quadruple O, and he made no attempt to pronounce the 'the' sound in the 'the'.

'Cooks to t'galley,' he said into the loudspeaker. 'Cooks to t'galley.'

The Paymaster Commander went back to the galley. In the hundreds of years of the history of the British Navy this meaning of the word 'cooks' had suffered a change. They were no longer the men who actually cooked the food of their respective messes; they were merely the men who, each on his appointed day, carried the food from the galley to the mess. Already they were assembling there; men from the six-inch turrets and men from the four-inch HA guns; men from the magazines and men from the engine-room – in every quarter of the ship one man knew that it was his duty, as soon as he heard 'cooks to the galley' piped, to come and fetch food for his mates who could not leave their stations. The Paymaster Commander watched the food being served out, from A mess right through the alphabet to

Z mess; from AA to ZZ, and then from AAA to EEE – food for five men, food for seven men, food for nine men, according to the number in each quarter; for each mess the food was ready stacked, and the Paymaster Commander nodded in faint self-approval as he saw how smoothly the arrangements were working over which he had sat up late on so many evenings. This was his own special plan, and he thought it improved on the system prevailing in other ships. It called for forethought and organization to feed six hundred men in half an hour, men who could not leave their guns, their gauges, or their instruments even for a moment while death lay only just beyond the horizon.

'I want those mess-traps brought back,' said the Paymaster Commander sharply, 'don't leave them sculling about on the decks.'

It was his duty to fill the bellies of his men, but at the same time it was his duty to safeguard Navy property. Just because a battle was being fought was no excuse for exposing crockery – even crockery of enamelled iron – to needless damage. The cooks had all left, and the Paymaster Commander picked up a sandwich and stood eating it, looking down at the galley party squatting on the decks spooning up soup into their mouths. Five minutes more of this let-up in the battle and everyone in the ship would have food inside him, and be fit and ready to go on fighting until nightfall or later.

He finished his sandwich and pulled out his cigarette case, and then stood with it unopened as a further thought struck him. He looked down fixedly at the Canteen Manager and his assistant.

'The boys'll want cigarettes,' he said. 'I expect half of 'em are short already.'

The Paymaster Commander was of the type that could use the word 'boys' instead of 'men' without being suspected of sentimentality.

'I expect so, sir,' said the Canteen Manager.

'Better take some round,' said the Paymaster Commander. 'You and Murchie see to it.'

'Aye aye, sir,' said the Canteen Manager, and then he hesitated. 'Shall I issue them, sir?'

'Issue them? Good God, no.'

The Paymaster Commander had visions of the endless reports and explanations he would have to make if he gave cigarettes away free to the Navy on the mere excuse that they were in action. And he had been in the service long enough to see nothing incongruous in the idea of sailors having to pay for their cigarettes in a ship which might during the next ten minutes be battered into a shapeless wreck.

'Half of 'em'll have no money, not after Alex, sir,' said the Canteen Manager.

'Well,' said the Paymaster Commander, the struggle between regulations and expediency evident in his face, 'let 'em have credit. See that every man has what he wants. And some of the boys'll like chocolate, I expect – take some round as well.'

The Paymaster Commander really meant 'boys' and not 'men' when he said 'boys' this time – there were plenty of boys on board, boys under eighteen, each with a sweet tooth and a growing frame which would clamour for sweetmeats, especially after the nervous strain of beating off aerial attack for four hours.

The 'mess-traps' about which he had worried – the 'fannies' of soup, the mugs and the plates – were already being returned to the galley. Things were going well. The Canteen Manager and his assistant filled mess-cans with packets of cigarettes and packets of chocolate, and began to make their way from action station to action station, selling their wares as though at a football match. Like the Paymaster Commander, neither the Canteen Manager nor the men saw anything incongruous in their having to put their hands into their pockets to find the pennies for their cigarettes and their bars of chocolate. It was a right and proper thing that they should do so, in fact.

'You men return to your action stations,' said the Paymaster Commander to the galley party.

He looked round the galley once more, and then turned away. He walked forward, stepped over the coaming, took one last glance backward at the blue sky and the grey sea, and then set himself to climb the dark ladders again back to the coding room. Even if he did nothing else in the battle he had supplied the food and the strength to keep the men going during a moment in the future when history would balance on a knife-edge – his forethought and his training and his rapid decision had played their part.

2

From the Captain's Report
. . . At 12.05 smoke was sighted . . .

Ordinary Seaman Harold Quimsby sucked a hollow tooth in which a shred of corned beef had stuck apparently inextricably. He ought to have reported that hollow tooth at least a month ago, but Quimsby was of the type of man who crosses no bridges until he comes to them. He did not let anything worry him very much, for he was of a philosophical nature, filled with the steady fatalism to be expected of a veteran of so much service, even though Quimsby was merely an enlistment for hostilities only. Some men would be uncomfortable up here in the crow's nest – not so Quimsby, whose ideal existence was one something like this, with a full belly and nothing particular to do. As HMS *Artemis* rolled and corkscrewed over the quartering sea the crow's nest swung round and round in prodigious circles against the sky, but Quimsby's seasoned stomach positively enjoyed the motion and untroubled went on with the process of digestion.

Cold meat and pickles; that made a meal fit for a king. Quimsby liked nothing better than that. His portion of pickles had included no fewer than four onions, and Quimsby breathed out reminiscently, conscious of, and delighting in, his flavoured breath. He had swallowed down his soup and his cocoa, but they were only slop, unworthy of the name of food. Cold meat and pickles were the food for a man. He sucked at his tooth again, and breathed out again, sublimely contented with the world.

Everything seemed to be designed for his comfort. The chair in which he sat certainly was – the padded seat and back held him in exactly the right position for keeping the horizon under continuous observation through the binoculars laid upon the direction finder before his eyes. As Quimsby rolled and circled round in the crow's nest he automatically kept the horizon swept by the binoculars; long practice had accustomed him to do so. A thrust of his feet one way or the other kept his stool rotating from port to starboard and back again, while his right hand on the lever kept the elevation in constant adjustment to correspond with the roll of the ship. Thanks to many hours of practice Quimsby was able to watch the whole horizon forward of the beam without allowing any of his automatic movements to break into his internal chain of thought, from the shred of beef in his tooth to the comfortable state of his inside and from that to unholy memories of that little bint at Alex who had made his last shore leave so lively.

And from there his memories went back to his first arrival at Alex, his first glimpse of the East, and from there to his first voyage to sea back in the almost unbelievably distant days of 1939. He had been up in the crow's nest then, too, he remembered and his forehead wrinkled in faint bewilderment at the certainty that the scared, sea-sick, self-conscious youth at the direction finder in those days was, unbelievably but beyond all doubt, the same man who sat there so self-assured and competent now. That first report he had to make, when his binoculars picked up the dot on the distant surface and he had rung down to the bridge, his stomach heaving with excitement and sea-sickness.

'Something over on the left,' he had spluttered, all his previous instruction forgotten.

The unhurried voice of the First Lieutenant had steadied him.

'Where are you speaking from?'

'Headmast – I mean masthead, sir.'

'Then that's what you say first, so that we know down here. And you don't say "over on the left", do you? What do you say?'

'On – on the port bow, sir.'

'That's right. But it's better to give a bearing. What does your bearing indicator read?'

'Twenty-one, sir.'

'And how do you say it?'

'I – I've forgotten, sir.'

'Port is red, and starboard is green,' said the First Lieutenant patiently. 'Remember that port wine is red, and then you won't forget. And twenty-one isn't plain enough, is it?'

'No, sir – yes, sir.'

'Now let's have your report. Remember to say where you're speaking from first.'

'M – masthead, sir. Object in sight. Red two-one.'

'Very good, Quimsby. But you must say it twice over. You remember being told that? If the guns are firing we might not hear you the first time.'

'Yes, sir. I mean aye aye, sir.'

He had been a very green hand at that time, decided Quimsby. He felt self-conscious all over again at the thought of how Number One had coaxed him into making his report in the proper form so that it could be instantly understood. The subject was almost unsavoury to him, and his thoughts began to drift farther back still, to the time when he was selling newspapers in Holborn – the evening rush, the coppers thrust into the one hand as with the other he whipped the copies out from under his arm.

Then he looked more attentively at the horizon, blinked, and looked again with his hand on the buzzer of the voice tube. Then he rang.

'Forebridge,' came the reply up the voice tube.

'Masthead. Smoke on the starboard bow. Green one-nine. Masthead. Smoke on the starboard bow. Green one-nine,' said Quimsby ungratefully, all memory of that early training passing from his mind as he said the words.

3

From the Captain's Report

. . . and a signal to this effect was immediately made . . .

In HMS *Artemis* a high proportion of the brains of the ship was massed together on the bridge, Captain and Torpedo Officer, Navigating Lieutenant and Officer of the Watch, Asdic cabinet and signalmen. They stood there unprotected even from the weather, nothing over their heads, and, less than shoulder-high round them, the thin plating which served only to keep out the seas when the ship was taking green water in over her bows. Death could strike unhindered anywhere on that bridge; but then death could strike anywhere in the whole ship, for the plating of which she was constructed was hardly thicker than paper. Even a machine gun bullet could penetrate if it struck square. The brains might as well be exposed on the bridge as anywhere else – even the imposing looking turrets which housed the six-inch guns served no better purpose than to keep out the rain. The ship was an eggshell armed with sledgehammers, and her mission in life was to give without receiving.

Was it Voltaire who said that first? No, it was Molière, of course. Paymaster Sub-Lieutenant James Jerningham, the Captain's secretary, was sometimes able to project himself out of the ship and look down on the whole organization objectively. It was he who was thinking about Voltaire and Molière as he squatted on the deck of the bridge eating his sandwich. Even after three years in the Navy he still had not learned to spend several hours consecutively on his feet the way these others did – they had learned the trick young (for that matter, save for the Captain, he was at twenty-seven the oldest officer on the bridge) and could stand all day long without fatigue. In the delirious days before the war he had written advertising copy, spending most of his time with his heels on his desk, and to this day he only felt really comfortable with his feet higher than his head.

One way of thinking of the ship was as of some huge marine animal. Here on the bridge was the animal's brain, and radiating from it ran the nerves – the telephones and voice tubes – which carried the brain's decisions to the parts which were to execute them. The engine-room was the muscles which actuated the tail – the propellers – and the guns were the teeth and claws of the animal. Up in the crow's nest above, and all round the bridge where the lookouts sat raking sea and sky with their binoculars, were the animal's eyes, seeking everywhere for enemies or prey, while the signal flags and the wireless transmitter were the animal's voice, with which it could cry a warning to its fellows or scream for help.

It was a nice conceit, all this; Jerningham summoned up all his knowledge of anatomy and physiology (he had spent hours with a medical dictionary when he wrote advertising copy for patent medicines) to continue it in greater detail. The ratings detailed as telephone numbers on the bridge and scattered through the ship, with their instruments over their ears, were the ganglia which acted as relay stations in the animal's nervous system. The rating who had just brought him his sandwich was like the blood vessel which carried food material from the galley – stomach and liver in one – to the unimportant part of the brain which he represented, to enable it to recuperate from fatigue and continue its functions.

The lower animals had important parts of their nervous systems dotted along their spinal cords – large expansions in the dorsal and lumbar regions to control the limbs. The Chief Engineer down in the engine-room would represent the lumbar expansion; the Gunnery Lieutenant in the Director Control Tower would be the dorsal expansion – the one managing the hind-limbs with which the animal swam, and the other the fore-limbs with which it fought. Even if the brain were to be destroyed the animal would still move and fight for a time, just as a headless chicken runs round the yard; and, like the very lowest animals, like the earthworm or the hydra, if the head were cut off it could painfully grow itself a new one if given time – the Commander could come forward from his station aft and take command, the Torpedo Gunner take the place of the Torpedo Lieutenant. And, presumably, young Clare would come forward to take his place if he, Jerningham, were killed.

Jerningham shuddered suddenly, and, hoping that no one had noticed it, he pulled out a cigarette and lit it so as to disguise his feelings. For Jerningham was afraid. He knew himself to be a coward, and the knowledge was bitter. He could think of himself as lazy, he could think of himself as an unscrupulous seducer of women, he could tell himself that only because of the absence of need he had never robbed the blind or the helpless, and it did not disturb his equanimity. That was how he was made, and he could even smile at it. But it was far otherwise with cowardice. He was ashamed of that.

He attributed to his brother officers a kindly contemptuous tolerance for the fear that turned his face the colour of clay and set his lips trembling. He could not understand their stolid courage which ignored the dangers around them. He could see things only too clearly, imagine them only too vividly. A bomb could scream down from the sky – he had heard plenty that morning. Or from a shadowy ship on the horizon could be seen the bright orange flare that heralded a salvo, and then, racing ahead of the sound they made would come the shells. Bomb or shell, one would burst on the bridge, smashing and rending. Officers and ratings would fall dead like dolls, and he, the Jerningham he knew so well, the handsome smiling Jerningham whose good looks were only faintly marred by having a nose too big for the distance between his eyes, would be dead, too, that body of his torn into fragments of red warm flesh hanging in streamers on the battered steel of the bridge.

Closing his eyes only made the vision more clear to Jerningham. He drew desperately on his cigarette although it was hard to close his lips round the end. He felt a spasm of bitter envy for the other officers so stolid and impassive on the bridge – the Captain perched on his stool (he was a man of sense, and had had the stool made and clamped to the deck to save himself from standing through the days and nights at sea when he never left the bridge). Torps and Lightfoot, the Officers of the Watch, chatting together and actually smiling. They had been unmoved even during the hell of this morning, when planes had come shrieking down to the attack from every point of the compass, and the ship had rocked to the explosion of near-misses and the eardrums had been battered into fatigue by the unremitting din of the guns.

Part of the explanation – but only part, as Jerningham told himself with bitter self-contempt – was that they were so wrapped up in their professional interests that their personal interests became merely secondary. They had spent their lives, from the age of thirteen, preparing to be naval officers, preparing for action, tackling all the problems of naval warfare – it was only natural that they should be interested in seeing whether their solutions were correct. And Jerningham had spent his years rioting round town, drinking and gossiping and making love with a gang of men and women whose every reaction he had come to be able to anticipate infallibly, spending first a handsome allowance from his father and then a handsome salary for writing nonsense about patent medicines. He had always felt pleasantly superior to those men and women; he had felt his abilities to be superior to those of any of the men, and he had taken to his bed any of the women he had felt a fancy for, and they, poor creatures, had been flattered by his attentions and mostly fallen inconveniently in love with him. It was humiliating to feel now so utterly inferior to these officers round him, even though war was their trade while he was merely a temporary officer, drifted into the rank of Paymaster Sub-Lieutenant and the position of Captain's secretary because for his own convenience he had once studied shorthand and typewriting. Those were happy years in which he had never felt this abasement and fear.

Jerningham remembered that in his pocket was a letter, unopened as yet, which he had picked up the day before when they left Alex, and which he had thrust away in the flurry of departure without bothering to open. It was a letter from that other world – it might as well be a letter from Mars, from that point of view – which ought to do something to restore his self-respect. It was in Dora Darby's writing, and Dora was nearly the prettiest, certainly the cleverest, and probably the woman who had been most in love with him of all that gang. She had written him heartbroken letters when he had first joined the Navy, telling how much she missed him and how she longed for his return – clever though she was, she had no idea that Dorothy Clough and Cicely French were receiving from him the same attentions as he was paying her. It would help to bolster up his ego to read what she had written this time, and to think that there were plenty of other women as well who would as eagerly take him into their arms. Only a partial compensation for this fear that rotted him, but compensation and distraction nevertheless. He opened the letter and read it – nearly six months old, of course, now that all mail save that by air was being routed via the Cape.

Dearest J. J.,

I expect you will laugh at what I have to tell you. In fact, I can just picture you doing so, but someone has to break the horrid news to you and I think I am the right person. The fact is that I am married!! *To Bill Hunt!!! I suppose it will seem odd to you, especially after what I've always said, but marriage is in the air here in England, and Bill (he is a First Lieutenant now) had a spot of leave coming to him, and we didn't see why we shouldn't. What will make you laugh even more is that Bill has been doing his best to get me with child, and I have been aiding and abetting him all I can. That is in the air too. And honestly, it means something to me after all these years of doing the other thing. And another thing is I shouldn't be surprised if Bill's efforts have been successful, although I can't be sure yet –*

Dora's letter trailed off after that into inconsequential gossip which Jerningham made no effort to read. That opening paragraph was quite enough for him; was far too much in fact. He felt a wave of hot anger that he should have lost his hold over Dora, even though that hold was of no practical use to him at the moment. It touched his pride most bitterly that Dora should have even thought of marrying a brainless lout like Bill Hunt, and that she should never have expressed a moment's regret at having to accept Bill as a poor sort of substitute for himself.

But this sort of jealousy was very mild compared with the other kind that he felt at the thought of Dora becoming pregnant. This simply infuriated him. He could not, he felt, bear the thought of it. And the brutal phrase Dora used – 'to get me with child' – why in hell couldn't she have worded it more gently? He knew that he had always coached Dora to call a spade a spade

– not that she needed much coaching – but she might have had a little regard for his feelings, all the same. Those pointed words conjured up in Jerningham's mind mental pictures as vivid as those of bombs dropping on the bridge. Dora and he and the others of his set – Bill among them, for that matter – had always assumed an attitude of lofty superiority towards people who were foolish enough to burden themselves with children and slack-fibred enough to lapse into domesticity; and in moments of high altruism they had always thought it selfish and unkind to bring a child into the sort of world they had to live in. And yet if anyone were going to 'get Dora with child', he wanted to do the job himself, and not have Bill Hunt do it. Up to this minute he had hardly even thought of marrying, far less of becoming the father of a family, and yet now he found himself bitterly regretting that he had not married Dora before *Artemis* left for the Mediterranean, and not merely married her but made her pregnant so that there would be a young Jerningham in England today.

He had never been jealous in his life before, and it hardly occurred to him that he had had almost no cause to be. He had always thought that he would smile a tolerant smile if one of his women before he had quite done with her should transfer her affections to someone else. But this was not the case, very much not the case. He was hot with anger about it, and yet the anger about this was merely nothing compared with his anger at the thought of Dora being made pregnant by Bill Hunt. His jealousy about this was something extraordinary. Jerningham found time even in the heat of his rage to note with surprise the intensity of his feelings on the subject; he had never thought for a moment, during the blasé twenties of his, that he would ever feel the emotions of uncultured humanity. For a harrowing moment he even began to wonder whether all his early cynicism had been quite natural to him. This was certainly the third instance of primitive emotion overcoming him – the first was away back in 1939, when he suddenly realized that Hitler was aiming at the enslavement of the world and he had found himself suddenly determined to fight, willing to risk even death and discomfort sooner than be enslaved; the second was when he had known physical fear, and this was the third time, this frightfully painful jealousy, this mad rage at being helpless here at sea while Bill Hunt enjoyed all the privileges of domesticity with Dora Darby. Self-analysis ceased abruptly as a fresh wave of bitter feeling swamped his reason.

He got on to his feet – he, who never stood when he could sit – because he simply could not remain physically quiescent while emotion banked up inside him. A buzz from the voice tube behind him made him swing round, and he took the message.

'Masthead reports smoke, green one-nine,' he sang out, his voice harsh and unwavering, as it would have been if it had been Dora Darby he had been addressing.

'Very good,' said the Captain, 'Chief Yeoman, make that to the flagship.'

4

From the Captain's Report

. . . Action was taken in accordance with the orders previously issued . . .

'So that's that,' said Captain the Honourable Miles Ernest Troughton-Harrington-Yorke to himself.

The signal flags were already racing up the halliards – the Chief Yeoman had begun to bellow the names of the flags before the last words of the order had left his lips. It would be the first warning to the Admiral that the possible danger which they had discussed previously was actually materializing. The Italian fleet was out, as the reconnaissance submarines had hinted; and if it was out it could be trusted to be out in full force. How many battleships they had managed to make seaworthy after Taranto and Matapan no British officer knew quite for sure, but now he would know. He would see them with his own eyes, for the Italians would never venture out except in the fullest possible force.

He twisted on his stool and looked round him over the heaving sea. Ahead of the *Artemis* stretched an attenuated line of destroyers, the destroyer screen to keep down possible submarines. Away to port lay the rest of the squadron of light cruisers; the light cruiser silhouette had altered less than that of any type of ship since

Jutland, and the ships looked strangely old-fashioned and fragile – mid-Victorian, to exaggerate – in their parti-coloured paint. The White Ensigns with the gay block of colour in the corner, and the red crosses, seemed somehow to accentuate this effect of fragility. Flown by a battleship the White Ensign conveyed a message of menace, of irresistible force; but in a light cruiser it gave an impression of jauntiness, of reckless daring, of proudly flaunting itself in the face of peril.

In the centre flew the Rear-Admiral's flag, beside the signal acknowledging that of the *Artemis*. The Captain wondered faintly what the Rear-Admiral was thinking about at this moment. Away over the port quarter wallowed the convoy, the fat helpless merchant ships, with a frail destroyer screen round them and the anti-aircraft cruiser in the centre. Helpless enough they looked, and yet they bore within them cargoes of most desperate urgency. Malta was threatened with every danger the imagination could conceive – the danger of attack from the air, of attack from the sea, of pestilence and of famine. A civilian population of a quarter of a million, and a garrison of God-only-knew how many were on short rations until the food these ships carried should be delivered to them. The anti-aircraft guns which took such toll of raiding aircraft were wearing their rifling smooth – here came new inner tubes to line them; and the barrages which they threw up consumed a ton of high explosive in five minutes – here were more shells to maintain those barrages. Here were heavy guns of position, with mountings and ammunition, in case the Italians should venture their fleet within range to cover a landing. Here were bandages and dressing and splints for the wounded, and medicines for the sick – the sick must be numerous, huddled below ground on meagre rations.

If the convoy did not get through Malta might fall, and the fall of Malta would mean the healing of a running ulcer which was eating into the strength of Mussolini and Hitler. And to escort the convoy through there were only these five light cruisers and a dozen destroyers – the convoy *had* to get through, and if it were reckless to risk it with such an escort, then recklessness had to be tolerated. The man over there whose Rear-Admiral's flag fluttered so bravely could be relied upon to be reckless when necessary; the Captain knew of half a dozen incidents in which the Rear-Admiral had displayed a cold-blooded calculation of risks and an unwavering acceptance of them. Wars could only be waged by taking chances; no Admiral since history began had ever been able to congratulate himself upon a prospective certainty. The Captain knew how the Admiral proposed to neutralize the chances against him, to counter overwhelming strength with overwhelming skill. The next few minutes would show whether his calculations would be justified.

'You can see the smoke now, sir,' said the Chief Yeoman of Signals.

There it was, heavy and black, on the horizon.

'Green one-o, sir,' said the forward lookout on the starboard side.

The big difference in the bearing proved that whatever it was which was making the smoke was moving sharply across the path of the squadron so as to head it off. The Captain turned and looked up at the vane on the mast, and at the smoke from the funnels of *Artemis*. It was only the slightest breath of smoke, he was glad to see – not the dense mass which the Italians were making, revealing their course and position half an hour before it was necessary.

He doubted if his smoke were visible even yet to the enemy, but it sufficed for his own purpose, which was to show him in what direction the wind was blowing. It was only a moderate breeze – last night's gale which had kicked up the present rough sea had died down considerably – and it was blowing from nearly aft. It was a strange turn of the wheel of fortune that the captain of a modern light cruiser on his way into action should have to bear the direction of the wind in mind and manoeuvre for the weather gauge as if he were the captain of one of Nelson's frigates. But the weather gauge would be of vital importance in this battle, and the squadron held it. The Italians had lost the opening trick, even though they held all the cards in their hands. And this moderate breeze was ideal for the laying of a smoke screen – not strong enough to disperse it, and yet strong enough to roll it down slowly towards the enemy. It was a stroke of good fortune; but the squadron needed all the good fortune there was available if it had to face the whole Italian navy. If the wind had been in any other direction – but yet the Admiral's orders had envisaged that possibility. There might have been some interesting manoeuvring in that case.

The Chief Yeoman of Signals was standing with his binoculars to his eyes, sweeping back and forth from the destroyers ahead to the flagship to port, but his gaze dwelt twice as long upon the flagship as upon all the other ships put together. For the Chief Yeoman, during the twenty-eight years of his service, had been in battles before, from the Dogger Bank to the present day, and he felt in his bones that the next signal would come from the flagship. The discipline and training of twenty-eight years, in gunboats on Chinese rivers, in battle cruisers in the North Sea, were at work upon him to catch that signal the moment it was hoisted, so that it did not matter to him that in addition his life might depend on the prompt obedience of the *Artemis*. He had stood so often, in peace and in war, ready to read a signal, that it was natural to him to ready himself in this fashion, as natural to him as breathing.

The wife he loved, back in England – the service had kept him apart from her during twenty of the twenty-five years of their married life – had been twice bombed out of her home, and all the furniture they had collected and of which he had been so modestly proud was now nothing but charred fragments and distorted springs; he had a son who was a Leading Seaman in one of the new battleships, and a daughter who was causing her mother a good deal of worry because she was seeing too much of a married man whom she had met in the factory. He was a living, sentient human being, a man who could love and who could hate, a man with a heart and bowels like any of his fellows, the grey-haired head of a household, an individual as distinct as any in the world, but at this moment he was merely the eye of HMS *Artemis* – less than that, a mere cell in the body of the marine creature which Jerningham had been visualizing, a cell in the retina of the creature's eyeball specialized to receive visual impressions.

'Signal from the Flag, sir,' said the Chief Yeoman of Signals, 'K for King.'

'Acknowledge,' said the Captain.

The cell in the retina had done its job, had received its visual impression and passed it on to the brain.

The Captain had open on his knee, already, the typewritten orders which laid down what each ship should do in certain specified circumstances, and he had foreseen that the present circumstances were those which would be covered by scheme K – moderate wind abaft, enemy to leeward. A pity in some ways, from the artistic point of view; there would have been some pretty work if it had been necessary to manoeuvre the Italians into the leegauge.

'Signal's down, sir,' said the Chief Yeoman.

'Port ten,' said the Captain. 'Two-one-o revolutions.'

'Port ten,' said the Navigating Lieutenant into the voice pipe, 'two-one-o revolutions.'

The moment when a signal is to be obeyed is the moment when it is hauled down; the squadron was moving out to defend the convoy from the Italian navy in the way that had been planned. The Captain swung his glasses round him; the convoy was executing a wheel to port under full helm, the cruisers were turning more gently and increasing speed so as to remain interposed between it and the enemy, and the destroyers in the advanced screen were doubling round, some to reinforce the immediate escort of the convoy in case of simultaneous aerial attack, some to clear the range for the light cruisers. It was a beautiful geometrical movement, like a figure in some complicated quadrille.

'Midships,' said the Captain.

'Midships,' repeated the Navigating Lieutenant into the voice pipe.

He broke the word into two, distinctly, for Able Seaman Dawkins was at the helm, perhaps the most reliable quartermaster in the ship's company, but once – during that night action – Dawkins had misheard the word and the Navigating Lieutenant was taking no chances in the future. The ship was steady on her course now.

Deep down in the ship, below the water line, where there was the least chance of an enemy's shell reaching him, Able Seaman Dawkins stood with his hands on the wheel and his eyes on the compass before him. With his legs spread wide he balanced himself with the ease of long practice against the roll of the ship; that had to be done automatically down here with no stable thing against which the movement could be contrasted, and with his eyes never straying from the compass. It was only a few minutes back – at noon – that he had come down here and taken over the wheel. He was comfortably full of food, and at the moment his cheek was distended and he was sucking rhythmically. A few years back one would have guessed at once that he was chewing tobacco, but with the new Navy one could not be sure – and in the present case one would have been wrong, for Dawkins was sucking a lollipop, a huge lump like yellow glass which he had slipped into his cheek before going below. He had a two-pound bottle of them in his locker, bought in Alexandria, for as Dawkins would have explained, he was 'partial to a bit of sweet'. One of those vast things would last him during nearly the whole of his trick at the wheel if he did not crunch down upon it when it began to get small.

At the time when he left the deck full of soup, cocoa, and sandwich, and with his lollipop in his cheek to top up with, the aerial attacks had ceased, and convoy and escort had been rolling along at peace with the world. While he had been eating his sandwich Brand had told him that there was a buzz that the Eyety navy was out, but Dawkins was of too stable a temperament to pay much attention. He was a man of immense placidity and immense muscle; in fact, as he stood there sucking on his lollipop one could hardly help being reminded of a cow chewing the cud. It was hard, studying his expressionless face and his huge hairy arms and hands, to credit him with the sensitive reactions necessary to keep a light cruiser steady on her course in a heavy sea. He stood there at the wheel, the two telegraph men seated one on each side of him; he towered over them, the three of them, in that small grey compartment, constituting a group which in its balance and dramatic force seemed to cry out to be reproduced in sculpture.

Above his head the voice pipe curved down at the end of its long course through the ship from the bridge; it, too, had a functional beauty of its own.

'Port ten, two-one-o revolutions,' said the voice pipe unexpectedly in the Navigating Lieutenant's voice; the sound came without warning, dropping into the silence of the compartment suddenly, as on a still day an apple may fall from a tree.

'Port ten, two-one-o revs, sir,' echoed Dawkins instantly, turning the wheel. At the same moment the telegraphman beside him spun the handle of the revolution indicator to two-one-o, and he was at once conscious of the faster beat of the ship's propellers.

A sudden change of course; a sudden increase of speed; that meant action was imminent, but Dawkins had no means of knowing what sort of action. It might be dive bombers again. It might be torpedo bombers. A submarine might have been sighted and *Artemis* might be wheeling to the attack, or the track of a torpedo might have been sighted and *Artemis* might be turning in self-defence. It might be the Eyety navy, or it might be trouble in the convoy.

'Midships,' said the voice pipe.

A man of less placid temperament than Dawkins might be irritated at that pedantic enunciation; the Navigating Lieutenant always pronounced the word that way, but Dawkins was philosophic about it, because it was his fault in the first place; once when he had had to repeat the word he had been caught transferring his lollipop from one cheek to the other and had spluttered in consequence, so that the Navigating Lieutenant believed his order had not been correctly heard.

'Midships,' repeated Dawkins; the ship was lying now much more in the trough of the waves, and he had to bring into play a new series of trained reactions to keep *Artemis* steady on her course. Those minute adjustments of the wheel which he was continually making nipped in the bud each attempt of wind and sea to divert the ship from the straight line; a raw helmsman would do nothing of the sort, but would have to wait for each digression to develop before recognizing it so that the ship would steer a zigzag course infuriating the men controlling the guns.

The guns were not firing yet, perhaps would not fire in this new action, but it would not be Dawkins's fault if they were incorrectly aimed, just as it would not be his fault if there were any time wasted at all between a decision to change course forming itself in the brain of the Captain and its being executed by the ship. He stood there by the wheel, huge and yet sensitive, immobile and yet alert, eyes on the compass, sucking blissfully on his lollipop, satisfied to be doing best the work which he could best do without further thought for the turmoil of the world outside.

5

From the Captain's Report

. . . an Italian force of two heavy cruisers of the 'Bolzano' type and four cruisers of the 'Regolo' type and 'Bande Nere' type.

Another signal ran to the masthead of the flagship, fluttered to await acknowledgement, and then descended.

'Starboard ten,' said the Captain, with the Navigating Lieutenant repeating the order, 'Midships.'

The squadron now was far ahead of the convoy, and lying a little way distant from a straight line drawn from the convoy astern to the tell-tale smoke ahead, ready at a moment's notice, that was to say, to interpose as might be necessary either with a smoke screen or with gunfire. Italians and British were heading directly for each other now at a combined speed of more than fifty miles an hour. It could not be long before they would sight each other – already the smoke was as thick and dense as ever it would be.

The masthead voice pipe buzzed.

'Forebridge,' said Jerningham, answering it, and then he turned to yell the message to the Captain. 'Ships in sight!'

As Ordinary Seaman Quimsby's binoculars picked

out more details he elaborated his reports with Jerningham relaying them.

'Six big ships!' yelled Jerningham. 'Six destroyers. Two leading ships look like battleships. Might be heavy cruisers. Others are light cruisers.'

The crow's nest where Quimsby swayed and circled above the bridge was twenty feet higher than the bridge itself. It was an easy calculation that Quimsby's horizon lay one and a half miles beyond the captain's, and that in two minutes or a little less the Italians would be in sight from the bridge. In two minutes they shot up suddenly over the curve of the world, climbing over it with astonishing rapidity. Visibility was at its maximum; they made hard, sharp silhouettes against the blue and grey background, not quite bows on to the British squadron, the ships ahead not quite masking the ships astern. Jerningham heard the voice of the rangetaker begin its chant, like a priest of some strange religion reciting a strange liturgy.

'Range three-one-o. Range three-o-five. Range three-double-o.'

There were other voices, other sounds, simultaneously. The ship was rushing towards a great moment; every cell in her was functioning at full capacity.

'Port fifteen,' said the Captain, and *Artemis* heeled over as she executed the sudden turn. 'Revolutions for twenty-seven knots.'

The squadron had turned into line ahead, and was working up to full speed to head off the Italians should it become necessary. As Jerningham watched the Italian ships he saw the leader turn sharply to starboard, revealing her profile; some seconds later the next ship turned to follow her, and then the next, and the next. Jerningham was reminded of some advertising display or other in a shop window. The vicious bad temper which Dora Darby's letter had aroused still endured within him, keying him up. The gap between imaginative fear and sublime courage, in a highly strung person, is only a small one; the residuum of bad temper sufficed to push Jerningham into boldness. He saw those six sharp profiles; the wind, blowing from the British to the Italians, kept them clear of smoke, unsoftened and undisguised. Jerningham went back through his memory, to those hours spent in his cabin of careful study of the pictured profiles of hostile ships, study carried out in a mood of desperate despair, when he knew himself to be a coward but was determined to be a coward deficient in nothing. He had the splendid memory which goes with a vivid pictorial imagination, and he could recall the very pages on which he had seen those profiles, the very print beneath them. He stepped forward to the Captain's side.

'The two leading ships are Bolzanos, sir,' he said. 'Nine thousand tons, eight eight-inch, thirty-two knots.'

'You're sure?' asked the Captain mildly. 'Aren't they Zaras?'

'No, sir,' said Jerningham with unselfconscious certainty. 'And the last three light cruisers look like Bande Neres. I don't know about the first one, though, sir. She's like nothing we've been told about. I suppose she's one of the new ones, Regolos, and the Intelligence people didn't get her profile right.'

'I expect you're right,' said the Captain. He had turned a little on his stool to look at Jerningham; he was surprised to see his secretary thus self-assured and well poised, for the Captain had seen his secretary in action before and had struggled against the suspicion that Jerningham had not all the control over his emotions which was desirable in the British Navy. But the Captain had learned to control his own emotions, and not the slightest hint of his surprise appeared in his expression or his voice.

'I think I am, sir,' said Jerningham, dropping back again.

In the Long Acre office he had had the ideal secretary, Miss Horniman, always at hand, always acquainted with the latest development, ready to remind him of the appointment he had forgotten or the copy he had to deliver, sympathetic when his head ached in the morning, and wooden faced and unassuming when she put forward to him an idea which he had not been able to produce, content that her boss should receive the credit that was rightfully hers. Jerningham always modelled his behaviour towards the Captain on Miss Horniman's behaviour towards him. The Captain might possibly have been wrong in his report of what he had seen if his secretary had not put him right, and the Captain would have the credit and the secretary would not, but that was the destiny, the proper fate of Captain's secretaries. He could grin to himself about that; the irony and incongruity of it all appealed to his particular sense of humour.

The Captain was a Captain RN; thought Jerningham, only a few grades lower than God; out of a hundred who started as naval cadets only very few ever reached that lofty rank – he was a picked man, with Staff College training behind him, but here was something his secretary could do better than he. It was a very considerable help to think about that; it saved Jerningham from some of the feeling of intense inferiority which plagued him.

But he respected the Captain none the less, admired him none the less. Jerningham looked at him in profile, with his glasses trained out to starboard on the Italian squadron. Those black eyebrows were turned up the tiniest trifle at the corners, giving him a faintly Mephistophelian appearance. It was a slightly fleshy face; the big mouth with its thick lips might well have been coarse if it had not been firmly compressed and helped out by the fine big chin. There was something of the artist about the long fingers which held the glasses, and the wrists were slender although muscular. Jerningham suddenly realized that the Captain was a slender man – he had always thought of him as big, powerful, and muscular. It was a surprise to him; the explanation must be that the Captain must have so much personality and force of character that anyone talking to him automatically credited him with physical strength.

It made more piquant still the sensation of discovering that the Captain had been in doubt of the identification of those Italian cruisers. Otherwise it would have been almost insufferable to see the steady matter of fact way in which the Captain looked across at the heavy odds opposed to him, the inhuman coolness with which he treated the situation, as if he were a spectator and not a participant, as if – what was certainly the case, for that matter – as if his professional interest in the tactics of the forthcoming battle, and his curiosity regarding what was going to happen, left him without a thought regarding his own personal danger.

Jerningham felt intense envy of the Captain's natural gifts. It was an envy which blended with, and fed, the fires of the jealousy which Dora Darby's letter had aroused in him.

6

From the Captain's Report

. . . At 1310 the enemy opened fire . . .

Captain Miles Ernest Troughton-Harrington-Yorke kept his glasses trained on the Italians. Jerningham was undoubtedly right about the identification of them. The six best cruisers the Italians had left; and that was a Vice-Admiral's flag which the leading ship was flying. They could not be more than a few hundred yards out of range, either, with those big eight-inch guns of theirs. The Captain looked to see them open fire at any moment, while the British six-inch still could not drop a shell within three thousand yards of them. With the very detailed reports which must have reached them from the air they could be in no doubt of the situation; they could fear no trap, have no doubt of their superiority of strength. It was possible – likely, in fact, in view of the other intelligence – that this Italian force was only a screen for a still stronger one, of battleships and more heavy cruisers, but there was no need to wait for reinforcements. They were strong enough to do the business themselves, two heavy cruisers and four light against five light cruisers.

Only two months ago the situation had been reversed, when *Artemis* and *Hera* had come upon that Italian convoy escorted by the two Italian destroyers. The disproportion of strength had not been very different. If the Italian destroyer captains had been realists they would have simply run away, and by their superior speed they could have saved their own ships while abandoning the convoy to destruction. But they had stayed to fight, like a couple of fools, advancing boldly towards the British cruisers, and endeavouring to lay a smoke screen. The first broadside of six-inch from *Artemis* had hit one of the destroyers – the Captain still felt intense professional pleasure at the recollection – and the third from *Hera* had hit the other. The two destroyers had been blown into flaming, sinking wrecks before even their feeble 120 mm guns had had a chance to fire; the British cruisers rushing down on them destroyed them in the few seconds which it took to cover the distance representing the difference in range. So the destroyers expended themselves uselessly, not having delayed for a moment the destruction of the transports they were escorting. Very foolish of them indeed.

If the Italian admiral over there – I wonder who he is? Nocentini, perhaps, or is it Pogetti? – knows his business he will turn two points to port and close with us and finish us off. And if we knew our business we would run like hares and save ourselves, and let the convoy go, and let Malta go.

The Captain's tightly shut mouth stretched into a dry grin. That was logic, but logic was not war. If it were, Hitler would be dining in Buckingham Palace this evening, and Napoleon would have dined there a hundred and forty years ago. No, that was a slipshod way of putting it. War was perfectly logical, but to grasp all the premises of war was very difficult and it was as fatally easy to draw incorrect conclusions from incomplete premises in war as in everything else. A mere count of the tonnage and the guns of the opposing sides was insufficient; it was even insufficient to include an estimate of the relative excellence of the training and discipline of the personnel on the two sides. There were other factors – the memory of Matapan, of Taranto, of the River Plate; the memory even of the defeat of the Spaniards of the Armada or of the defeat of the Italians at Lissa eighty years back.

The Captain had read somewhere of an unpleasant child who used to find amusement in chasing the slaves round the compound with a hot poker. The child found out quite early that it was unnecessary to have the poker actually red hot; it would serve just as well if it were painted so that the slaves thought it was hot. The slaves might even suspect that it was only painted, but they would not take the chance involved in finding out. So it was at the present moment; the British Navy had a record of victory over odds, and the Italians one of defeat by inferior numbers. This time the Italians might suspect that the odds were too heavy, the numbers too inferior, for history to repeat itself. But it might call for more resolution than they possessed to put the matter to the proof. It was going to be interesting to see.

Something beautiful showed itself at that moment in the field of the Captain's binoculars, a tall, lovely column of water, rising gracefully out of the sea like the arm clothed in white samite, mystic, wonderful, which rose from the mere to catch Excalibur. The Captain had vague theories of beauty; he had often wondered why one curve should be more beautiful than another, one motion more graceful than another. But he had never tried to crystallize his theories, to give definition to what he felt might be indefinable. Hogarth had once attempted it, with his 'Line of Beauty' on the palette depicted in the corner of his self-portrait, and he had tried again, and failed disastrously, when he wrote his 'Analysis of Beauty'.

But for all that, it might be worth someone's while to try to analyse why the column of water thrown up by an eight-inch shell should be so beautiful. The rate of its rise (and the mathematics of the relative velocities of its constituent particles had their own charm as well) the proportion of height to girth, the very duration of its existence, were all so perfectly related to each other as to give pleasure to the eye. The faint yellow tinge that it possessed (that meant high explosive shell) was an added charm against that sky and sea. And farther away, to left and to right, rose its fellows at the same moment, each as beautiful as the other; they were widespread, and even allowing for the fact that those eight-inch were firing at extreme range that meant that the gunnery control instruments in the Italian ship were not lined up as carefully nor as accurately as they should be.

The leading ship was altering round towards the enemy. That was the way to deal with them; if they won't come and fight, go in and fight them.

'Starboard ten,' said the Navigating Officer into the voice tube, as *Artemis* reached the position where each of her four predecessors had made their two-point turns, and the cruiser heeled again as the rudder brought her round.

7

From the Captain's Report

. . . the enemy withdrew . . .

All down the line of Italian cruisers ran a sparkle of light, bright yellow flashes competing with faint success against the sunlight. Leading Seaman Alfred Lightfoot saw the flashes in the cruiser upon which he was training his rangefinder; he saw them double, because the rangefinder presented two images of the cruiser, just overlapping. That double image was something like what he had seen once or twice halfway through a binge, after the seventh drink or so. For a few minutes, then, the lights behind the bar, and the barmaid's face, duplicated themselves in just the same fashion, just as substantially, so that one could swear that the girl had two faces, one overlapping the other by half, and that each electric bulb had another hung beside it.

Lightfoot twirled the controlling screws of the rangefinder, and the two images moved into each other; in the same way, when Lightfoot was getting drunk, he could by an effort make the two images of the barmaid's face run together again, so that they would click into sharp unity instead of being hazy and oreoled with light. He read off the scale of the rangefinder.

'Range two-seven-ho,' he announced, his Cockney

twang flavouring the dry tone in which he had been trained to make his statements; the vowel sound of the word 'range' was exactly the same as he would have used in the word 'rind'.

The sharp image at which he was peering was obscure again at once; two shadowy cruisers were replacing the single one – there were two red, white and green flags flying aft, a muddled double mass of funnels. With his Cockney quickness of thought Lightfoot could, if he had wanted to, have drawn the obvious conclusion, that the two squadrons were approaching each other rapidly, and he could from there have gone on to the next deduction, which was that in a very few seconds they would be pounding each other to pieces. But Lightfoot did not trouble to think in that fashion. Long ago he had told himself fatalistically that if a shell had his name on it he would cop it, and from no other shell. His job was to take ranges quickly and exactly; that was to be his contribution to the perfect whole which was the fighting ship, and he was set upon doing that without distraction. Just once or twice when he had strayed into self-analysis Lightfoot had felt a little pleased with himself at having attained this fatalistic Nirvana, but it is hard to apportion the credit for it – some of it was undoubtedly due to Lightfoot himself, but some also to the system under which he had been trained, some to the captain for his particular application of that system; and possibly some to Mussolini himself, who had given Lightfoot a cause in which to fight whose justice was so clearly apparent.

Lightfoot twisted the regulating screws again to bring the images together. It was twenty-one seconds since he had seen the flashes of the guns of the cruiser at which he was pointing, and Lightfoot had already forgotten them, so little impression had they made upon him. And during those twenty-one seconds the eight-inch shells had been hurtling towards *Artemis* at a speed through the air of more than a mile in two seconds because their path was curved, reaching far up into the upper atmosphere, higher than the highest Alps into the freezing stratosphere before plunging down again towards their target. Lightfoot heard a sudden noise as of rushing water and of tearing of sheets, and then the field of his range finder was blotted out in an immense upheaval of water as the nearest shell of the broadside pitched close beside starboard bow of *Artemis*. Twenty tons of water, yellowed slightly by the high explosive, came tumbling on board, deluging the upper works, flooding over Lightfoot's rangefinder.

'Ringe hobscured,' said Lightfoot.

He reached to sweep the lenses clear, and darkness gave way to light again as he stared into the instrument. For a moment he was still nonplussed, so different was the picture he saw in it from what he had seen just before. The images were double, but the silhouettes were entirely changed, narrow instead of broad, and the two flecks of colour, the double images of the Italian flag, were right in the middle of each silhouette instead of aft of them. Lightfoot's trained reactions were as quick as his mind; his fingers were spinning the screws round in the opposite direction at the same moment as he realized that the Eyeties had turned their sterns towards the British and were heading for the horizon as fast as they could go.

The spectacle astonished him; the surprise of it broke

through his professional calm in a way in which the prospect of danger quite failed to do.

'Coo!' said Lightfoot; the exclamation (although Lightfoot did not know it) was a shortening of 'Coo blimey', itself a corruption of 'God blind me'.

'Coo!' and then instantly training and professional pride mastered him again, and he brought the images together with a deft twirl of the screws 'Range two-nine-ho'.

Paymaster Sub-Lieutenant James Jerningham saw the Italian ships turn away, and he gravely noted the time upon his pad. One of his duties was to keep a record of any action in which the ship was engaged, because experience had proved that after an action, even with the help of the ship's plot which was kept up to date in the chart-room, and with the help of the various logs kept in different parts of the ship – signal logs, engine-room logs, and so on – it was difficult for anyone to remember the exact order of events as they had occurred. And reports had to be written, and the lessons of the action digested, if only for the benefit of the vast fleet in all the oceans of the world anxious to improve its professional knowledge.

The Captain slid down from his stool and stretched himself; Jerningham could tell just from his actions that he was relieved at not having to sit for a while – the lucky devil did not know that he was well off. Jerningham's feet ached with standing and he would have given something substantial in exchange for the chance to sit down. The Captain walked briskly up and down for a while, five paces aft and five paces forward; the bridge was too small and too crowded with officers and instruments to allow of a longer walk. And even during that five-pace walk the Captain kept shooting glances round him, at signalmen and flagship and lookouts so as to maintain himself in instant readiness for action.

It might be said that while the ship was at sea the Captain never went more than five paces from his stool; at night he lay on an air mattress laid on the steel deck with a blanket over him, or a tarpaulin when it rained. Jerningham had known him to sleep for as much as four hours at a stretch like that, with the rain rattling down upon him, a fold of the stiff tarpaulin keeping the rain from actually falling on his face. It was marvellous that any man could sleep in those conditions; it was marvellous that any man bearing that load of responsibility could sleep at all; but, that being granted, it was also marvellous that a man once asleep could rouse himself so instantly to action. At a touch on his shoulder the Captain would raise his head to hear a report and would issue his orders without a moment in which to recover himself.

The Captain was tough both mentally and physically, hard like steel – a picked man, Jerningham reminded himself. And no man could last long in command of a light cruiser in the Mediterranean if he were not tough. Yet toughness was only one essential requisite in the make-up of a cruiser captain. He had to be a man of the most sensitive and delicate reflexes, too, ready to react instantly to any stimulus. Mere vulgar physical courage was common enough, thought Jerningham, regretfully, even if he did not possess it himself, but in the Captain's case it had to be combined with everything else, with moral courage, with the widest technical knowledge, with flexibility of mind and rapidity of thought and physical endurance – all this merely to command the ship in action, and that was only part of it. Before the ship could be brought into action it had to be made into an efficient fighting unit. Six hundred officers and men had to be trained to their work, and fitted into the intricate scheme of organization as complex as any jigsaw puzzle, and, once trained and organized, had to be maintained at fighting pitch. There were plenty of men who made reputations by successfully managing a big department store; managing a big ship of war was as great an achievement, even if not greater.

Jerningham, with nearly three years of experience, knew a great deal about the Navy now, and yet his temperament and his early life and his duties in the ship still enabled him to look on the service dispassionately as a disinterested observer. He knew better than anyone else in the ship's company how little work the Captain seemed to do when it came to routine business, how freely he delegated his power, and having delegated it, how cheerfully he trusted his subordinates, with none of those after-thoughts and fussinesses which Jerningham had seen in city offices. That was partly moral courage, of course, again, the ability to abide by a decision once having made it. But partly it was the result of the man's own ability. His judgement was so sound, his sense of justice so exact, his foresight so keen, that everyone could rely on him. Jerningham suspected that there might be ships whose captains had not these advantages and who yet were not plagued with detail because officers and men united in keeping detail from them knowing that the decisions uttered would not be of help.

Those would be unhappy ships. But the kind of captain under which he served was also not plagued with detail, because officers and men knew that when they should appeal to him the decisions that would be handed down to them would be correct, human, intelligent. In that case officers and men went on cheerfully working out their own destiny, secure in the knowledge that there was an ability greater than their own ready to help them should it become necessary. That would mean a happy, efficient ship like *Artemis*.

Jerningham's envy of the Captain's capacity flared out anew as he thought about all this. It was a most remarkable sensation for Jerningham to feel that someone was a better man than he – Jerningham's sublime egotism of pre-war days had survived uncounted setbacks. Lost games of tennis or golf, failure to convince an advertising manager that the copy laid before him was ideal for its purpose, could be discounted on the grounds of their relative unimportance, or because of bad luck, or the mental blindness of the advertising manager. In this case there was no excuse of that sort to be found. Jerningham had never yet met an advertising manager whose work he did not think he could do better himself; the same applied to office heads – and to husbands. But Jerningham had to admit to himself that the Captain was better fitted than he was to command a light cruiser, and it was no mitigation that he did not want to command a light cruiser.

To recover his self-respect he called back into his mind again the fact that he had been quicker than the Captain in the identification of the Italian cruisers, and he went on to tell himself that the Captain would not stand a chance in competition with him for the affections of the young women of his set, with – not Dora Darby (Jerningham's mind shied away from that subject hastily) – but with Dorothy Clough or Cicely French, say. That was a comforting line of thought. The Captain might be the finest light cruiser captain, actual or potential, on the Seven Seas – Jerningham thought he was – but he was not to compare with Jerningham in anything else, in the social graces, or in appreciation of art or literature. The man had probably never seen beauty in anything. And it was quite laughable to think of him trying to woo Cicely French the way Jerningham had, finding her in a tantrum of temper, and subtly coaxing her out of it with womanish sympathy, and playing deftly on her reaction to win her regard, and telepathically noting the play of her mood so as to seize the right moment for the final advance. The very thought of the Captain trying to do anything like that made Jerningham smile through all his misery as he met the Captain's eye.

The Captain smiled back, and stopped in his walk at Jerningham's side.

'Was it a surprise to you, their running away like that?' asked the Captain.

Jerningham had to think swiftly to get himself back on board *Artemis* today from a Paddington flat three years ago.

'No, sir,' he said. 'Not very much.'

That was the truth, inasmuch as he had had no preconceived tactical theories so as to be surprised at all.

'It may be just a trick to get us away from the convoy,' said the Captain. 'Then their planes would have a chance. But I don't think so.'

'No, sir?' said Jerningham.

'There's something bigger than cruisers out today, I fancy. They may be trying to head us into a trap.'

The Captain's eye was still everywhere. He saw at that moment, and Jerningham's glance following him saw too, the flagship leading around in a sixteen-point turn.

'Starboard fifteen,' said the Navigating Lieutenant, and the deck canted hugely as *Artemis* followed her next ahead round. She plunged deeply half a dozen times as she crashed across the stern waves thrown up first by her predecessors and then by herself, and white water foamed across her forecastle.

'Flagship's signalling to convoy, sir,' said the Chief Yeoman of Signals, '"Resume previous course".'

'We're staying between the Eyeties and the convoy,' remarked the Captain, 'and every minute brings us nearer to Malta.'

'Yes, sir,' said Jerningham. He cast frantically about in his mind for some contribution to make to this conversation other than 'Yes, sir,' and 'No, sir.' He wanted to appear bright.

'And night is coming,' said Jerningham, grasping desperately at inspiration.

'Yes,' said the Captain. 'The Eyeties are losing time. The most valuable asset they have, and they're squandering it.'

Jerningham looked at the Satanic eyebrows drawing together over the curved nose, the full lips compressed into a gash, and his telepathic sympathies told him how the Captain was thinking to himself what he would do if he commanded the Italian squadron, the resolution with which he would come plunging down into battle.

And then the eyebrows separated again, and the lips softened into a smile.

'The commonest mistake to make in war,' said the Captain, 'is to think that because a certain course seems to you to be the best for the enemy, that is the course he will take. He may not think it the best, or there may be some reason against it which you don't know about.'

'That's true, sir,' said Jerningham. It was not an aspect of war he had ever thought about before; most of his thoughts in action were usually taken up by wondering what his own personal fate would be.

Ordinary Seaman Whipple was climbing the difficult ladder to the crow's nest to relieve the lookout there. The Captain allowed himself to watch the changeover being effected, and Jerningham saw him put back his head and inflate his chest to hail the masthead, and then he relaxed again with the words unspoken.

'And the next commonest mistake,' grinned the Captain, 'is to give unnecessary orders. Whipple up there will keep a sharp lookout without my telling him. He knows that's what he's there for.'

Jerningham gaped at him, wordless now, despite his efforts to appear bright. This was an aspect of the Captain's character which he had never seen before, this courteous gentleman with his smiling common sense and insight into character. It crossed Jerningham's mind, insanely at that moment, that perhaps the Captain after all might be able to make some progress with Cicely French if he wanted to.

8

From the Captain's Report

. . . the enemy's cruisers were then joined by a fresh force consisting of two battleships of the 'Littorio' class and another cruiser of the 'Bolzano' class . . .

Ordinary Seaman Albert Whipple was a crusader. Like most crusaders he was inclined to take himself a little too seriously, and that made him something of a butt to his friends. When he took over from Quimsby the latter grinned tolerantly and poked him in the ribs while pointing out to him the things in sight – the smoke of the Italian cruiser squadron, and their funnels just visible over the horizon, the distant shapes of the convoy wallowing doggedly along towards Malta.

'An' that thing in the front of the line is the flagship,' concluded Quimsby with heavy-handed humour. 'Give my regards to the Admiral when you get your commission.'

For one of the theories that the lower deck maintained about Whipple's seriousness was that he wanted promotion, aspiring to the quarterdeck, for Whipple had a secondary school education. The lower deck was wrong about this. All that Whipple wanted to do was to fight the enemy as efficiently as was in his power, in accordance with the precepts of his mother.

Albert was the youngest of a large family, and his elder brothers and sisters were quite unlike him, big and burly, given to the drinking of beer and to riotous Saturday nights; they had all gone out to work at fourteen, and it was partly because of the consequent relief to the family finances that Albert had been able to set his foot on the lower rungs of the higher education. The brothers and sisters had not objected, had shown no jealousy that the youngest should have had better treatment than they; in fact, they had been mildly proud of him when he came home and reported proudly that he had won the scholarship which might be the beginning of a career. Albert was white-faced and skinny, like his mother, and desperately serious. The brothers and sisters had never paid any attention to their mother's queer behaviour; their work in the tannery and the toy factory had made them good union members, but they had no sympathy with her further aspirations, with her desperate interest in the League of Nations, in the Japanese invasion of China and Franco's rebellion in Spain. They had laughed, as their father had learned to do before they were born. Their father could remember as far back as 1914, when the eldest child – George – was on the way, finding her standing on the kerb watching the soldiers of the new army marching down the street, bands playing and people cheering, and yet she had tears running down her cheeks at the sight of it. Mr Whipple had clapped her on the back and told her to cheer up, and as soon as George was born had gone off and joined the army and had done his bit in Mespot. And when he had come back, long after the war was over, he had found her all worked up about the Treaty of Versailles, and when it was not the Treaty of Versailles it was some new worry about the Balkans or the militarization of the Rhine or something.

She had tried to capture the interest of each of her children in turn regarding the problems of the world, and she had failed with each until Albert began to grow up. He listened to her; it was a help that during his formative years he came home to dinner while the rest ate sandwiches at the factory. Those *tête-à-têtes* across the kitchen table, the skinny little son listening rapt to the burning words of his skinny little mother, had had their effect. Albert had it in mind when he was still quite young that when he grew up it would be his mission to reform the world; he was a little priggish about it, feeling marked out from the rest of humanity, and this conception of himself had been accentuated by the fact that unlike his brothers and sisters he had started a secondary education, and that he passed, the summer in which war began, his school examination a year younger than the average of his fellows and with distinctions innumerable.

The brothers had joined the Air Force or the Army, but with pitiably small sense of its being a sacred duty; they did not hold with Hitler's goings on, and it was time something was done about it, but they did not think of themselves as crusaders and would have laughed at anyone who called them that. And Albert had stayed with his mother, while his father worked double shifts at the tannery, until after a few months Albert and his mother talked over the fact that now he was old enough to join one of the Services at least – a poster had told them how boys could join the Royal

Navy. Mrs Whipple kept back her tears as they talked about it; in fact, she jealously hugged her pain to her breast, womanlike. At the back of her mind there was the thought of atonement, of a bloody sacrifice of what she held dearest in the world, to make amends for her country's earlier lethargy and indifference. She was giving up her best loved son, but to him she talked only of his duty, of how his call had come to him when he was hardly old enough for the glory of it. And Albert had answered the call, and his confident certainty in the rightness of his mission had carried him through homesickness and seasickness, had left him unspotted by his messmates' spoken filth and casual blasphemies. He had endured serenely their amused tolerance of his queer ways and priggish demeanour, and he devoted himself to the work in hand with a fanaticism which had raised the eyebrows of the petty officers of HMS *Collingwood* so that now he was Ordinary Seaman in *Artemis* and noted down in the Commander's mental books – and in those of the Captain, too – as certain to make a good Leading Seaman in time.

Sea service weathered his complexion to a healthy tan, but neither good food nor exercise had filled him out at all. Perhaps the thought of his mission kept him thin. He was still hollow-cheeked, and his comparatively wide forehead above his hollow cheeks and his little pointed chin made his face strangely wedge-shaped, which intensified the gleam in his eyes sunk deep under their brows. All his movements were quick and eager; he grabbed feverishly at the binoculars resting in their frame before his face, so anxious was he to take up his duties again, to resume his task of avenging Abyssinia and hastening the coming of the millennium. Lying in a hospital at that moment, her legs shattered by the ruins that a bomb from a German aeroplane had brought down, his mother was thinking of him, two thousand miles away; either through space or through time it was her spirit which was animating him.

Whipple searched the horizon carefully, section by section, from the starboard beam to right ahead and then round to the port beam and back again; there was nothing to report, nothing in sight beyond what Quimsby had pointed out to him. He swivelled back again to the Italian squadron; his hatred might have been focused through lenses and prisms like some death-dealing ray, so intense was it. There were only the funnels of the cruisers to see, and the pall of smoke above them stretching back behind them in a dwindling plume. He swivelled slowly forward again, and checked his motion abruptly. There was a hint of smoke on the horizon at a point forward of the Italians, almost nothing to speak of, and yet a definite trace of smoke, all the same, and clearly it was no residual fragment of the smoke of any of the ships which Whipple had in sight. For five seconds Whipple watched it grow before he pressed the buzzer.

The Captain's secretary answered it – a man Whipple had never cared for. He suspected him of he knew not what, but he had also seen him drunk, only just able to stagger along the brow back into the ship, and Whipple had no use for a man who let himself get drunk when there was work to be done, while there was a mission still unfulfilled. But Whipple did not allow his dislike to interfere with his duty. If anything, it made him more careful than ever with his enunciation, more painstaking to make an exact report of what he could see.

'Forebridge,' said Jerningham.

'Masthead. More smoke visible on the port bow,' said Whipple pedantically. 'Beyond the enemy cruisers. Green three-eight.'

He repeated himself just as pedantically. Back through the voice pipe, before Jerningham closed it, he could hear his report being relayed to the Captain, and that gave him the comforting assurance that Jerningham had got it right. He swept the horizon, rapidly and thoroughly, before looking at the new smoke again; it was always as well to take every possible precaution. But there was nothing further to report except as regards the new smoke. He pressed the buzzer again.

'Masthead,' he said. 'The new lot of smoke is closing us. The same bearing. No, green three-nine.'

A bigger wave than usual, or a combination of waves, lifted *Artemis* ten feet vertically at the same moment as beyond the horizon another combination of waves lifted the Italian battleship *Legnano* ten feet also. In that crystal clear air against the blue sky, Whipple caught a glimpse of solid grey – funnel tops and upperworks, the latter apparently the top storey of a massive gunnery control tower. It came and went almost instantaneously, but Whipple knew what it was, and felt a wave of fierce excitement pass over him like a flame. Yet excitement could not shake the cold fixity of his purpose to do his duty with exactitude.

'Masthead,' he said down the tube, dryly and unemotionally. 'Battleship in sight. Green four-o.'

The blood was pulsing faster in his veins. A bibliophile finding in the twopenny box a long-sought first edition would know nearly the same thrill as Whipple felt, or a knight of the Round Table at a vision of the Grail. There were thousands of Italians there to be killed, ships which were the pride of the Italian navy were there to be destroyed. 'The thicker the hay,' said Alaric once, when the odds against his army were being pointed out to him, 'the easier it is mown.' 'The bigger they come,' said Bob Fitzsimmons, 'the harder they fall.' Whipple thought along the same lines. The appalling strength of the hostile force meant nothing to him, literally nothing, from the point of view of frightening him. He was merely glad that the enemy were presenting themselves in such numbers to be killed. If at that moment some impossible chance had put Whipple without time for reflexion in command of the English squadron, the light cruisers would have dashed headlong into action and destruction. But Whipple was not in command. He was perfectly conscious that he was merely the masthead lookout in HMS *Artemis*, and as such a man with a definite duty to perform to the best of his ability.

'Two battleships and a heavy cruiser,' he reported down the voice pipe, 'heading a little abaft our beam. On the same bearing now as the other ships. The other ships are turning now astern of them.'

Whipple was reporting the development of the Italian fleet into line of battle, and in exactly the same tone as he would have used if he had been reporting sighting a buoy. That was the contribution he was privileged to make to the cause his mother had talked about to him over the midday dinner table in Bermondsey. Ordinary Seaman Albert Whipple, aged eighteen, was a prig and a self-righteous one. A cynic might well define *esprit de corps* as self-righteous priggishness – the spirit which inspired Sir Richard Grenville or Cromwell's Ironsides. From the yardarm close beside Whipple fluttered the signal flags which he had set a-flying.

9

From the Captain's Report

. . . the behaviour of the ship's company was most satisfactory . . .

The Italian fleet was up over the horizon now, their upper works visible under the smoke, and the British squadron had wheeled about once more. The Italians were heading to interpose between the convoy and Malta; if it were not for that slow, lumbering convoy, crawling along at its miserable eleven knots, the light cruisers could have circled round the Italian battleships like a hawk round a heron. As it was the British squadron was like a man with a cannon ball chained to his leg, crippled and slow, forced to keep its position between the convoy and the Italian warships – those battleships were designed for twenty-nine knots and even when mishandled were quite capable of twenty-five. They could work steadily ahead, until they barred the route, forcing the British to attack to clear the path – as if a man with a penknife could clear a path out of a steel safe – and if the British sensibly declined the attempt and turned back, they would be pursued by the Italians, whose superior speed would then compel the light cruisers either to stay and be shot at or move out of the Italian path and leave the convoy to destruction.

It was all perfectly logical, positive, and inevitable when the data were considered – the eleven-knot convoy, the thirty-knot battleships, the Italian fifteen-inch guns, the British six-inch; the four hours remaining of daylight and the extraordinary clearness of the air. Fog might save the English, but there was no chance of fog in that sparkling air. Nightfall might save the English, too, for it would be most imprudent for battleships to engage in a night action with cruisers – that would be like staking guineas against shillings in a game of pitch-and-toss. But it was still early afternoon, and no more than half an hour would be needed for the Italians to reach their most advantageous position. Then five minutes of steady shelling would be sufficient to sink every cruiser in the British line; less than that to destroy the helpless convoy. Then Malta would fall; the running ulcer in Italy's side would be healed; Rommel in Africa, the submarines in the Atlantic would feel an instant lessening of the strain upon them; the Vichy government would be informed of one more step towards the German conquest of the world; the very Japanese in seas ten thousand miles away would be aware of a lightening of their task.

So obvious and logical was all this that the inferences must be clear to the rawest hand anywhere in the ship. It was not necessary to have studied Mahan, or to have graduated from the Staff College, to understand the situation. The ship's company of *Artemis* might not stop to think about Vichy or Rommel or the Japanese; but they knew the speed of the convoy, and the merest whisper of the word 'battleships' would tell them that their situation was a perilous one. And a mere whisper – with implied doubt – would be far more unsettling than any certainty. Not one man in ten in *Artemis* could see what was going on, and in a ship at action stations it was hard for information to filter through by word of mouth.

In the Captain's opinion distorted news was dangerous. He knew his men, and he believed that his men knew him; if they heard the truth he could rely upon them whatever the truth might be. A crisis in the battle was close at hand, and he could spare not one moment from the bridge to tell them himself. He turned a little on his stool, caught Jerningham's eye, and beckoned to him. Jerningham had to wait a second or two while the Captain brought himself up to date again regarding the situation, looking at flagship and convoy and enemy, before he took the glasses from his eyes and turned a searching glance at his secretary. Jerningham was acutely conscious of that glance. He was not being sized up for any trifle; it was not as if he was a mere applicant for a job in a City office. The business he was to do was something touching the whole efficiency of the ship – the safety of Malta – the life or death of England. The Captain would not have trusted him with it if he were not absolutely sure of him. In fact, the Captain was faintly surprised at finding that he *was* sure of him; he wondered a little whether he had previously misjudged his secretary or whether the latter was one of those people who had moods, and was sometimes reliable and sometimes not. But whether he had misjudged him or not, and whether he had moods or not, this was the right time to impose responsibility upon him and to make amends if he had misjudged him, or to give him confidence in the future if this was merely an exalted mood.

'Go down,' said the Captain, 'and tell the ship about the situation.'

Jerningham stood a little startled, but the Captain already had his binoculars to his eyes again. He had given his order, and an order given by a Captain in a ship of war is carried out.

'Aye aye, sir,' said Jerningham, saluting as he jerked himself out of his surprise.

He turned away and started down the ladder. He was an intelligent man, accustomed in his private life to think for himself, accustomed to selling ideas to advertising managers, accustomed to conveying ideas to commercial artists, accustomed to telling the public truths or fictions in the fewest and clearest words. The Captain might easily have expanded the brief order he gave his secretary, telling him what to say and how to say it, but the Captain knew that it was not necessary; and also that to leave the responsibility to his secretary would be good for him.

Jerningham's mind was feverishly turning over words and phrases as he descended the ladder; he did not have time to assemble any, but, on the other hand, he did not have time in those few seconds to become self-conscious, nor had his weakness time to reassert itself.

'I've a message for the ship from the Captain,' he said to the bosun's mate beside the loudspeaker bolted to the bulkhead.

The petty officer switched on and piped shrilly, the sound of his call audible in every part of the ship.

'The Captain has sent me to tell you,' said Jerningham to the mouthpiece, 'we've got the Eyety navy in front of us. Battleships, heavy cruisers, and all. They've run away from us once, the heavy cruisers have. Now we're going to see if the battleships'll run too. Three hours of daylight left, and the convoy's *got* to reach Malta. Good luck to us all. There's none like us.'

Jerningham opened his mouth to say more, but his good judgement came to his rescue and he closed it again. He had said all there was to say, and in an illuminated moment he knew that anything he were to add would be not only superfluous but possibly harmful. Men of the temper of the crew of *Artemis* did not need rhetoric; a plain statement of the facts for the benefit of those men below decks who had no idea what was happening was all that was needed.

He turned away from the unresponsive instrument, not knowing whether he had done well or badly; in the days of wooden ships, before public address systems had even been heard of, his words might have been received with cheers – or boos – which would have been informative. The ludicrous thought crossed his active mind that it was just like an advertising problem. How often had he devised ingenious methods by which to 'key' advertisements to discover which had the greateat pulling power?

His eyes met those of the bosun's mate, and then travelled on to exchange glances with the other ratings – messengers and resting lookouts – stationed here. One or two of the men still wore the expression of philosophic indifference which so often characterized the lower deck, but there was a gleam in the eyes of the others, a smile at the corners of their mouths, which told him that they were excited, and pleasurably excited. That telepathic sympathy of his, which had assisted him to the downfall of so many young women, made him aware that the men were feeling the same inconsequent exhilaration as he felt – inconsequent to him, and novel and strange, but something they had known before and recognized. A climax was at hand, the climax to months and years of training and forethought, to the unobtrusive mental conditioning for which the Mephistophelian Captain on the bridge was responsible, to the life's mission to which men like Ordinary Seaman Albert Whipple had devoted themselves, or to the long line of fighting ancestors, which had generated them – like A. B. Dawkins down at the wheel, whose great-great-grandfather had run with powder charges over the bloody decks of the *Temeraire* at Trafalgar. It was the prospect of such a climax which exhilarated them, just as, ridiculously, it exhilarated him, and left them all careless of any possible consequences to themselves. He ran up the steep ladder again to the bridge, disregarding the way in which it swayed and swung to the send of the sea.

10

From the Captain's Report

. . . increasing speed and at the same time making smoke . . .

Back on the bridge, Jerningham looked round him to see that there had been no radical change in the situation during the short time of his absence. There were the minutest possible dots on the horizon below the Italian funnel smoke which showed that the Italian fleet was now actually in sight. A new string of flags was breaking out on the halliards of the flagship.

The Captain knew this was the moment. The Admiral had let them round until they were properly stationed with regard to the wind which now blew in a line from them to a point ahead of the Italians – that blessed wind, of such a convenient strength and from such a convenient quarter – and he had timed his arrival in this situation at the very moment when the Italians would be almost within range with their fourteen-inch guns. And so far the Admiral had shown none of his hand, except to display a determination to yield nothing without fighting for it, and the Italians must have been expecting that at least, as was proved by their caution in bringing up their battleships only behind a heavy force of cruisers.

The Chief Yeoman of Signals interpreted the flagship's signal, and the Captain was ready for it – the plan which he held on his knee laid it down as the next step.

'Revolutions for thirty-one knots,' he ordered. 'Make smoke.'

The Navigating Lieutenant repeated the order, and the Officer of the Watch pressed the plunger which ordered smoke.

Down in the engine-room the Commander (E) stood on the iron grating; being a tall man the top of his head was no more than a few inches below the level of the sea. He stood there with the immeasurable patience of his breed, acquired during countless hours of standing on countless gratings, and with his feet apart and his hands clasped behind him in the attitude he had first been taught as a cadet eighteen years before. He was the supreme lord of this underworld of his, like Lucifer, and he seemed marked out as such by the loneliness of his position, without a soul within yards of him, and by the light-coloured boiler suit which he wore, and by the untroubled loftiness of his expression. The very lighting of the engine-room by some strange chance accentuated the fact, glaring down upon his face and figure with a particular brightness, specially illuminating him like a character on the stage. He was a young man to have the rank of Commander and to carry the responsibilities of his position, to have hundreds of men obedient to him, to have sixty-four thousand horse-power under his control, to be master of the pulsating life of a light cruiser, but it would be a hard task to guess his age, so deliberate were his movements and so unlined and yet so mature was his face.

All the Commander (E) had to do was to stand there on the grating and do nothing else. A crisis might be at hand, but it could not affect the Commander (E) unless some catastrophe occurred. His work was done for the moment; it had been accomplished already during the years *Artemis* had been in commission. He had trained the engine-room complement into complete efficiency – the Engine-room Artificers and the Mechanicians and the Stokers; the Lieutenants and Sub-Lieutenants (E) who were his heads of department and his subordinates – not so many years younger than he – loved him as if he were their father, and would have found it hard to explain why if called upon to do so. None could appreciate the magic serenity, that endless patience, who had not served under him. Because of the love they bore him they knew his will without his expressing it, and they laboured constantly to anticipate it, to perfect themselves in their duty because he wished it, so that the organization and routine of the engine-room ran as smoothly and as efficiently as did the turbines at that moment.

And the turbines ran smoothly because of the previous labours of the Commander (E) – the sleepless vigilance which had watched over material and supplies, had read every engine-room log, had studied the temperatures of every bearing, the idiosyncrasies of every oil jet. There had been the endless desk-work, the reports written to the Admiralty (the strange gods of Whitehall whose motives had to be guessed, and who had to be propitiated by exact and complicated paper ceremonial, but who, once propitiated, were lavish like the savage rain gods of Africa), the statistics to be gathered and studied, the plans that had to be made against future contingencies. In time of war a light cruiser repairs and reconditions when she can and not when she should; and the Commander (E) had had to use forethought, and had had to display prompt decision, deciding what should be done, what opportunities snatched at, what might safely be postponed, anticipating future needs, doing today what would have to be done anyway during the next two weeks, leaving until some uncovenanted future doing the things which were not immediately essential.

As a result of all this the Commander (E) had nothing to do now; everything was being done by itself. Even the Senior Engineer, Lieutenant (E) Charles Norton Bastwick, felt a lack of anything to do, and came lounging up to take his stand beside the Commander (E), hands behind him, feet apart, in the 'at ease' position; it would be some minutes before he would once more feel the urge to walk round again, reading gauges and thermometers, and thereby debarring the Commander (E) from doing the same. It would only be if an emergency arose – if some near-miss shook up a condenser so that it leaked, or if a torpedo hit flooded a compartment, or some similar damage was inflicted – that they would have their hands full, improvising and extemporizing, toiling along with their men to keep the ship afloat and the propellers turning. And if the ship were to meet her death, if the sea were to come flooding in and the scalding steam – steam as hot as red-hot iron, steam that could roast meat to a frizzled brown – should pour into boiler-room and engine-room, and the order 'abandon ship' should be given, they would be the last of all to leave, the last to climb the treacherous iron ladders up to sea level and possible safety.

The engine-room was hot, because the ship had been going twenty-seven knots for some time now. The thermometer on the forward bulkhead registered 105 degrees, but for an engine-room, and according to the ideas of men accustomed to working in one, that was not really hot. And the place was full of noise, the high-pitched note of the turbines dominating everything – a curious noise, in its way an unobtrusive noise, which sounded as if it did not want to call attention to itself, the loudest whisper one could possibly imagine. The ears of a newcomer to the engine-room would be filled with it, all the same, so that he could hear nothing else. Only after long experience would he grow so accustomed to the noise that he could distinguish other noises through it, and hear human voices speaking at their normal pitch. Until that should come about he would see lips move and not be able to understand a word.

Bastwick and the Commander (E) were aware that above them, on the surface of the sea some sort of action was taking place. All through the forenoon they had heard the four-inch and the Oerlikons and the pompoms firing in savage bursts, and they had known that the convoy and escort were under aerial attack; but then the guns fell silent over their heads, and food had been brought to them, and there had been a brief moment of tranquillity. But then the bridge had rung down for twenty-seven knots, and they had had to switch over from the cruising turbines to the main engines (that blessed fluid flywheel which made the changeover so rapid and easy!) and the ship had begun rapid manoeuvring. Since then course had been altered so often that it was hard to reconstruct the situation in the mind. And once the ship had rolled and quivered to an explosion close alongside – God only knew what that was, for not a gun had been fired in the ship since the morning.

The squeal of the bosun's pipe suddenly made itself heard through the loudspeaker in the engine-room, attracting everyone's attention to Jerningham's voice which followed it. 'We've got the Eyety navy in front of us . . . now we're going to see if the battleships'll run too . . .' Jerningham's voice came to an end, but the Commander (E) and Bastwick still stood at ease on the iron grating, unmoved and unmoving. At any moment a fifteen-inch shell might come crashing through the deck above them, to burst in the engine-room and rend the ship apart while dashing them to atoms. Around them and beneath them a thousand-odd tons of fuel oil awaited the chance to burst into flame and burn them like ants in a furnace. A hundred tons of high explosive, forward and aft, needed only to be touched off.

But it was of the essence of life down here below the protective deck that destruction might come at any second, without any warning at all, and – more important from the point of view of mental attitude – without any possibility of raising a hand to ward it off. There was nothing to do but one's duty, just as the comic poet once declared that he had nothing to eat save food. Down there Jerningham's announcement on the loudspeaker had the effect of making everyone feel a little superior to the world above them, as the white settlers in Africa in time of drought might watch the natives sacrificing chickens or dancing wild dances to bring rain; the whites could feel contemptuous or compassionate – but they could not make it rain any more than the natives could. Above decks, Jerningham's announcement was like a stone dropped into a pool, sending a ripple of excitement over the surface; below them it was like a stone dropped into treacle, absorbed without any apparent reaction. The Commander (E) and Bastwick were watching Engine-room Artificer Henrose making the routine test of the boiler water, making sure that under the stress of continuous high speed the sea water pumped through the condenser to cool the used steam and to make it available for reuse was not leaking through any one of the thousand joints. Henrose, balancing against the roll of the ship, held the test-tube of boiler water in his left hand and poised the bottle of silver nitrate over it, letting the reagent fall into it drop by drop. Jerningham's announcement made itself heard, but Henrose might just as well not have heard it as far as any apparent reaction was concerned. He levelled the bottle of silver nitrate, squinted at the test-tube, and shook it, and squinted again. There was not the slightest trace of the white precipitate of silver chloride which would indicate that there was salt in the boiler water – salt which would eat through joints and tubes and cripple the ship in a few hours. Henrose went swaying back along the heaving grating to spill out the test-tube of water and replace the silver nitrate bottle. Italian dreadnoughts might be within range; that was interesting, just as was the fact that Henry VIII had six wives, but there was no salt in the boiler water, and it was that which mattered.

To starboard and port the needles of the revolution indicators moved sharply round the dial; the Commander (E) from where he stood – he stood there because although he had ostensibly nothing to do he could see from there, everything of importance – could see that the number of revolutions ordered would give the ship thirty-one knots, full speed save for a knot or two in hand for emergencies. The Commander (E) was serenely aware that there was ample pressure available to satisfy this demand; it was because he could foresee such demands and plan economically for them ahead of time that he held the rank of Commander.

The four ratings who stood at the valves admitting steam to the four turbines began to spin the valves open, turning the horizontal wheels while watching the restless needles – two black and one red – of the dials. The note of the turbines began unbelievably to rise, unbelievably because the ear would not have believed that there could be a note higher than the previous one. More and more steam poured into the turbines, a tremendous torrent of steam, steam with a strength of sixty thousand horse-power. The beat of the propellers quickened, the needles crept farther round the dials until they caught up with and rested upon the others. The orders from the bridge were obeyed; the ship was making thirty-one knots, and in the engine-room it felt as if she were leaping like a stag from wave to wave over the lively sea.

A fresh noise broke through the whine of the turbines; this time it was a loud imperious clatter that none could mistake. A red light glowed high up on the bulkhead, and an indicator hand moved across from

'Stop making smoke' to 'Make smoke'. Bastwick moved forward leisurely towards the boiler-room. He knew that the signal was being repeated there – during the night before he had personally tested every communication – and he knew that Stoker Petty Officer Harmsworth was perfectly reliable, but he knew, too, that nothing is certain in war. As he went through the double door his ears clicked with the rise in pressure; at thirty-one knots the furnaces burnt in a few minutes enough oil fuel to warm the average house for a whole winter, and the air to consume that oil was a rushing mighty tempest dragged into the boiler-room by the partial vacuum set up by the combustion.

Harmsworth was completing the adjustment of the valves admitting just too much oil and shutting off just too much air to allow of complete combustion in this furnace. Bastwick stooped and peered through the glazed peephole. Normally it gave a view of a white-hot whirl of flame, but now it showed a hideous gloomy blackness; some of the oil was being burnt, but only just enough to break down the remainder into thick black greasy hydrocarbons whose sooty smoke was being caught up in the draught and poured through the after-funnel.

'Very good,' said Bastwick, straightening up.

The heat in here was oppressive, and the temperature would rise still higher with this increase in speed; there were trickles of sweat down Harmsworth's bull neck and among the hairs of his bare chest. Bastwick looked round the boiler-room, nodded to Sub-Lieutenant (E) Pilkington, and got a grin back in return. Pilkington was a brilliant youngster; one of these days he would be an Admiral. Bastwick completed a brief inspection and found everything satisfactory as it would be with Pilkington there. Then Bastwick made his way back to the engine-room, where the Commander (E) still stood on the iron grating, his handsome ageless face lit up by the harsh electric bulbs like that of a marble saint. But Bastwick knew that the Commander (E) had taken note that he, Bastwick, had recently inspected the boiler-room. The rudder indicator on the bulkhead, below the smoke telegraph, showed that the ship was changing course, and the two red lights beside it confirmed it by showing that the steering engines were at work. Bastwick knew, too, that the Commander (E) had noted this fact as well, and was making deductions from it regarding the battle. The saint might appear lost in contemplation, but when, or if, an emergency should arise he would be as prepared to deal with it as he could be, as any man could be.

II

From the Captain's Report

. . . I found the smoke screen to be extremely effective . . .

Artemis was flying through the water now; at that speed with the wind abeam and the sea nearly so she lurched savagely and with unremitting regularity, hitting each wave as if it were something solid, her forecastle awash with the white water which came leaping over her port bow. Last of the line, she tore along over a surface already whipped creamy white by the four ships ahead of her; the mountainous waves thrown up by five hulls each of nearly six thousand tons travelling at that speed diverged on either side of her and broke into white water where they crossed the waves thrown up by the destroyers racing in a parallel line. The five cruisers went tearing along in their rigid line. Smoke began to pour from the after-funnel of the flagship in the van, a wisp or two at first, and then a thick greasy never-ending cloud; within two seconds of the first wisps there was smoke pouring from the after-funnels of all five of them – five thick cylinders of smoke, each so dense as to appear liquid rather than gaseous. They drooped down to the surface of the sea, and rolled over it, pushed gently by that convenient wind towards the enemy, and hardly dissipating at all, spreading just enough to blend with each other in a wide bank of smoke diagonal to the squadron's course so that even the second ship in the line, to say nothing of *Artemis* at the rear, was completely obscured from the sight of the Italians. And the thirty-one knots at which the squadron was moving was far faster than anything the dreadnoughts could do, so that although the Italian fleet was faster than the convoy the smoke screen was being laid between the two; to attack the convoy the battleships would still have to come through the screen – they could not work round the end of it.

But to lay a smoke screen and to hide behind it was mere defensive warfare of the most pusillanimous kind. The enemy must be smitten, and smitten again, even though the smiting was with mere six-inch guns against twelve inches of armour-plate. Even though the enemy could not be hurt, his resolution must be broken down, his nerve shattered; he must be taught the lesson that he could not venture out to sea without submitting to vicious attack. And *Artemis* was last of the line of cruisers; abeam of her the smoke lay thickest, and it would be her movements that would be the most unpredictable to the enemy. It was her duty to smite, even though to smite she must expose those eggshell sides of hers to the sledgehammer blows of the enemy, and run the gauntlet of one-ton shells hurled with the velocity of a meteor, with an accuracy which could hit a tennis court from ten miles distance.

The Captain sat on the stool which bucked beneath him like a playful horse; the motion was unnoticed by him even though the reflexes developed during years at sea were continually at work keeping him steady in his seat. He was thinking deeply, but on subjects so logical, and with such a comforting ingredient of mathematics, that his expression gave no sign of it. The Mephistophelian eyebrows were their normal distance apart; and although the plan he was to carry out called for the highest degree of resolution, the firm mouth was no more firmly compressed than usual, for the plan was a part of the Captain's life, something he was going to do, not something he wished to do or did not wish to do; something the advisability of which was not in doubt even though the details of execution had had to be left to this last moment for consideration because of possible freaks of weather or possible unexpected moves on the part of the enemy.

Three minutes of smoke meant a smoke bank a mile and a half long, far too wide for the enemy to watch with care all along its length. And with the smoke being continually added to at one end, the other end would probably not be under observation at all. And the smoke bank, allowing for spread, would be a quarter of a mile thick, but *Artemis* would be going through it diagonally, and it would take her (the Captain solved a Pythagorean problem in his head) fifty-five seconds to emerge on the other side, without allowing for the drift of the bank before the wind. This fifteen-knot breeze added a refreshing complication to the mathematics of it. It would take over two minutes to traverse the smoke bank; two minutes and ten seconds. The Captain turned to the voice pipe beside him.

'Captain – Gunnery Officer,' he said. The Gunnery Lieutenant answered him.

'I am turning to starboard now, Guns. It will take us two minutes and ten seconds approximately to go through the smoke. You'll find the Eyeties about red five when we come out, but I shall turn to port parallel to their course immediately. Open fire when you are ready. All right? Goodbye.'

Artemis was the last ship in the line, and consequently the first to take action independently of the rest of the squadron.

'Turn eight points to starboard, Pilot,' he said to the Navigating Lieutenant.

'Starboard fifteen,' said the Navigating Lieutenant down the voice pipe; *Artemis* leaned far over outwards as she made the right-angle turn – full speed and plenty of helm. 'Midships. Steady!'

'Stop making smoke,' ordered the Captain; he wanted the range clear for the guns when he emerged, and the signal went down through five decks to Stoker Petty Officer Harmsworth in the boiler-room.

So far the wind had been carrying the smoke solidly away to starboard, but now *Artemis* was heading squarely into it. One moment they were out in the clear sunshine with its infinite visibility. The next moment they were in reeking darkness. The stink of unburnt fuel oil was in their nostrils and their lungs. It made them cough. And in the smoke it was dark, far darker than the darkest coloured spectacles would make it; the Captain looked round, and he could only just see the white uniform of the Navigating Lieutenant two yards away. It was most satisfactory smoke as far as he could tell – he looked aft towards the masthead and could see nothing. But there was just the chance that the mast was protruding through the smoke and betraying the movements of the ship to the Italians.

'Call the masthead and see if the lookout is in the smoke,' ordered the Captain, and Jerningham obeyed him.

'Masthead lookout reports he is in the smoke and can't see anything,' he called into the darkness when he had received Ordinary Seaman Whipple's reassurance.

The duty had been useful to him. When they had plunged into the smoke his heart had seemed to rise in his throat, and it was only with an effort that he had seemed to swallow it down. It was beating fast, and the beating seemed to find an echo in his finger tips so that they shook. But the distraction of having to speak to Whipple had saved him, and he was able to recapture his new found sang-froid.

'Thirty seconds,' said the Torpedo Lieutenant. He had switched on the light at the hooded desk and, stooping with his face close down, he was reading the movement of the second-hand of the deck-watch.

'Forty-five seconds.'

It was strange how silent the ship seemed to be, here in the smoke. The sound of the sea overside was much more obvious than out in the sunshine. Within the ship as she pitched over the waves, vibrating gently to the thrust of the propellers, there was a silence in seeming accord with the gloomy darkness that engulfed them. The Captain knew that darkness did not necessitate absence of noise; it was a curious psychic phenomenon this assumption that it was quieter. No, it was not. In the smoke or out of it the wind was still blowing, and the turn which *Artemis* had just made had brought the wind abaft when before it was squarely abeam. That accounted for it; the ship really was quieter.

'One minute,' said the Torpedo Lieutenant.

That was interesting, to discover that it had taken him fifteen seconds to make that deduction about the wind. The opportunity of honestly timing mental processes came quite rarely. And the study of the speed of thought was an important one, with its bearing on the reaction times of officers and men.

'Seventy-five seconds,' said the Torpedo Lieutenant.

He must remember, when he thought about this later, that at the moment he was keyed up and as mentally active as he well could be. Perhaps the brain really did work more quickly in those circumstances, although it was hard to imagine the physiological and anatomical adjustments which such a theory could postulate.

'Ninety seconds,' said the Torpedo Lieutenant.

Presumably the RAF doctors had been on a similar track for years. He must remember at some time or other to find out how much they had discovered; but they would of course be more interested in split seconds than in reactions lasting a quarter of a minute.

'One-o-five seconds,' said the Torpedo Lieutenant.

Not long to go now. But the smoke was just as thick as ever – extremely good. He must remember to put that in his report. The Captain shifted in his position on the stool, poising himself ready for instant action. It seemed to him as if the smoke were thinning. Just possibly the Italians could see by now the shadowy grey form of the *Artemis* emerging.

'Two minutes,' said the Torpedo Lieutenant.

Yes, he could see the Navigating Lieutenant plainly now. There was a second of sunshine, and then darkness again, and then they were out of the smoke, blinded a little by the sun, but not so blind as to be unable to see, full and clear, within six-inch gun range, the massive silhouettes of the Italian battle line almost right ahead of them, every detail plain, the complex gunnery control towers, the tripod masts, the huge guns, the reeking funnels.

'Port fifteen,' said the Captain, and *Artemis*, beautiful in the sunshine, swung round to turn her broadside upon that colossal force, like Ariel coming out to combat a horde of Calibans.

12

From the Captain's Report
. . . fire was opened . . .

The Gunnery Lieutenant wore the ribbon of the DSC on the breast of his coat. *Artemis* had won victories before, and, under the Captain, it was to the Gunnery Lieutenant's credit that those victories had been so overwhelming. There was the daylight action against the Italian convoy, when the first broadside which he had fired had struck home upon the wretched Italian destroyer which was trying to lay a smoke screen, had blown the destroyer into a wreck, and had enormously simplified the problem of the destruction of the convoy. The night action against another convoy had in certain respects been simpler, thanks to the Italians. They had not been so well trained, and because of their long confinement in harbour they had not had nearly as much experience at sea as the British. They had failed to spot *Artemis* in the darkness, and the Captain had been able to circle, to silhouette the Italians against the declining moon, and to creep up to them with guns trained and ready until they were within point-blank range at which no one could have missed. Two broadsides for one destroyer – the sheets of flame which engulfed her must have killed the men running to their guns, for she never fired a shot in return – and then a quick training-round and another broadside into the other destroyer. The latter actually fired in return, but the shells went into the sky; apparently her guns were trained ready for anti-aircraft action and some startled person just fired them off. Then nothing more from that destroyer after the second broadside crashed into her; only the roaring orange flames and the explosion of shells and torpedoes as the fire reached them and her crew roasted.

But at least *Artemis* had hit, with every broadside she had fired, and the loftiest gunnery officer in the British Navy could not have done better than that. It was proof at least that her gunnery was efficient, her gun crews fully trained, her infinite instruments properly adjusted, her gunnery officer steady of nerve and hand. In itself that was in no way enough to merit a decoration – it was no more than was expected of him – but the Admiralty must have decided that there was something more of credit to be given him, so that now he wore that blue-and-white ribbon.

Today the Gunnery Lieutenant's heart was singing. He was big and burly and fair. Perhaps in his veins there coursed some of the blood of a berserker ancestor; always at the prospect of action he felt this elation, this anticipation of pleasure. He felt it, but he was not conscious of it, for he was not given at all to self-analysis and introspection. Perhaps if someone whom he respected called his attention to it he would recognize it, this rapture of the strife, although years of schooling in the concealment of emotion would make the discovery a source of irritation. He was clear-headed and fierce, a dangerous kind of animal, employing his brain only along certain lines of thought. The men who swung the double axes beside Harold at Hastings and the reckless buccaneers who plundered the Spanish Main in defiance of odds must have been of the same type. With a Morgan or a Nelson or a Wellington or a Marlborough to direct their tireless energy and their frantic bravery, there was nothing that could stand against them.

It was tireless energy which had brought the Gunnery Lieutenant his present appointment. Not for him was the profound study of ballistics, or patient research into the nature of the stresses inside a gun; more clerkly brains than his could correlate experimental results and theoretical data; more cunning minds than his could devise fantastically complicated pieces of apparatus to facilitate the employment of the latent energy of high explosive. For the Gunnery Lieutenant it was sufficient that the results and the data had been correlated, that guns had been built to resist the stresses, that the apparatus for directing them had been invented. Dogged hard work – like that of an explorer unrelentingly making his way across a desert – had carried him through the mathematics of his gunnery courses and had given him a thorough grounding in the weapons he was to use. He knew how they worked – let others bother their heads about why they did. He had personality and patience enough to train his men in their use; the fiddling tiny details of maintenance and repair could be entrusted to highly skilled ratings who knew that their work was to stand the supreme test of action and that in the event of any failure they would have to face the Gunnery Lieutenant's wrath. Endless drills and battle practice had trained both the Gunnery Lieutenant and his men until he and they and the guns worked as a single whole, the berserker now instead of with the double axe was armed with weapons which could strike at twelve miles, could pull down an aeroplane six miles up.

He sat in the Gunnery Control Tower which he had not left since dawn, one knee crossed over the other and his foot swinging impatiently. His big white teeth champed upon the chocolate with which he stuffed his mouth; he was still hungry despite the vast sandwich which the Paymaster Commander had sent up to him, and the soup, and the cocoa. Indeed, it was fortunate that the Canteen Manager had made his way up to him and had sold him that chocolate, for the exertions of the morning had given the Gunnery Lieutenant a keen appetite, partly on account of the irritation he experienced at being on the defensive. Beating off aeroplane attacks, controlling the four-inch AA fire, was strictly defensive work and left him irritable – and hungry.

The opening moves of the battle on the surface mollified him to some extent. He admired the neat way in which the Admiral had parried the first feeble thrust of the Italians, and reluctantly he agreed that it was all to the good when the Italian cruiser screen withdrew after having done nothing more than pitch a few salvoes into the sea alongside the British ships. His ancestors had been lured out from the palisade wall at Hastings in a mad charge which had left them exposed to William the Conqueror's mailed horsemen; but the Gunnery Lieutenant, as one of the Captain's heads of department, had been for some time under a sobering influence and had been kept informed as to the possibility of Italian battleships being out. And he was aware of the importance of the convoy; and he was a veteran of nearly three years of life and death warfare. He had learned to wait cheerfully now, and not to allow inaction or defensive war to chafe him too much. But all the same the laying of the smoke screen, which (after all those careful conferences) he knew to be the first move in a greater game brought him a great upsurge of spirits. He listened carefully to what the Captain told him on the telephone.

'Aye aye, sir.'

Then *Artemis* leaned over outwards as she turned abruptly and plunged into the smoke screen.

In the Director Control Tower it remained bright; the smoke found it difficult to penetrate into the steel box, and the electric bulbs were continuously alight. The Gunnery Lieutenant's steel and leather chair was in the centre of the upper tier; on his right sat the spotting officer, young Sub-Lieutenant Raikes, binoculars poised before him, and on his left Petty Officer Saddler to observe the rate of change of range. In front of him sat Chief Petty Officer O'Flaherty, the Irishman from Connaught, at the director, and below him and before him sat a whole group of trained men, the pick of the gunnery ratings – picked by the Gunnery Lieutenant and tried and tested in battle and in practice. One of them was Alfred Lightfoot, his brows against the rubber eyepiece of his rangefinder; in the other corner was John Oldroyd, who had spent his boyhood in a Yorkshire mine and was now a rangetaker as good as Lightfoot. Behind them were the inclinometer operator and the range-to-elevation-and-deflection operator; the latter was a pop-eyed little man with neither chin nor dignity, his appearance oddly at variance with his pompous title, but the Gunnery Lieutenant knew him to be a man who did not allow himself to be flurried by danger or excitement. He was of the prim old-maidish type who could be trusted to keep his complex instrument in operation whatever happened, just as the Gunnery Lieutenant's maiden aunts kept their skirts down come what might. Even the telephone rating, his instrument over his head, had been hand-picked; in the ship's records he was noted as having been a 'domestic servant', and he found his present task of keeping track of telephone calls a little like his pre-war job when as a bachelor's valet he had had to converse over the telephone with creditors and relations and women friends and be polite to all of them. He had acquired then a rather pompous manner which stood him in good stead now in action – he had learned to recall it and employ it at times of greatest stress.

'We shall be opening fire on the enemy,' said the Gunnery Lieutenant into the telephone which connected him with the turrets, 'on a bearing about green eight-five.'

Long ago the Transmitting Station had passed the order 'all guns load', and before that the guns' crew had been in the 'first degree of readiness'. The team in the Director Control Tower, the marines stationed in the Transmitting Station, the men at the guns, were like men down on their marks waiting for the pistol before a sprint race. They would have to be off to a quick start – it would be on the start that everything would depend, because they must hit the enemy and get away again before the enemy could hit them back. Everybody in the ship knew that. Everybody in the ship had contributed something to the effort of making the thing possible, and now it was up to the gunnery men to carry the plan to completion.

Sunshine flicked into the Director Control Tower, flicked off again, and then shone strongly.

'Green five,' said the Spotting Officer as he caught sight of the Italian fleet, but the bearing changed instantly as *Artemis* swung round on a course parallel to the Italians.

'Fire at the leading ship,' said the Gunnery Officer, coldly brave. That was a battleship, least vulnerable of all to *Artemis*'s fire, but she flew the flag of the Italian Admiral. The three rangefinders in the ship were at work on the instant: Lightfoot and Oldroyd and their colleague Maxwell at the after-rangefinder spinning the screws and, as the double image that each saw resolved itself into one, thrusting with their feet at the pedals before them. Down in the Transmitting Station a machine of more than human speed and reliability read off all three recordings and averaged them. Each of the other observers in the Director Control Tower was making his particular estimate and passing it down to the Transmitting Station, and down there, by the aid of these new readings, the calculation having been made of how distant the Italian flagship was at that moment, other machines proceeded to calculate where the Italian flagship would be in fifteen seconds' time. Still other machines had already made other calculations; one of them had been informed of the force and direction of the wind, and would go on making allowance for that, automatically varying itself according to the twists and turns of the ship. Because every gun in the ship had its own little peculiarities, each gun had been given its individual setting to adjust it to its fellows. Variations in temperature would minutely affect the behaviour of the propellant in the guns, which would in turn affect the muzzle velocities of the shells, so that one machine stood by to make the corresponding corrections; and barometric pressure would affect both the propellant and the subsequent flight of the shells – barometric pressure, like temperature, varied from hour to hour and the Transmitting Station had to allow for it. And the ship was rolling in a beam sea – the Transmitting Station dealt with that problem as well.

'Table tuned for deflection, sir,' said the telephone to the Gunnery Lieutenant.

'Broadsides,' said the Gunnery Lieutenant coldly again. That was the way fighting madness affected him, so that he would take the wildest risks with the calmest manner.

All the repeaters before him had stopped moving now, and at this moment the last 'gun ready' lamp came on. There was no need to report to the Captain and ask permission to open fire; that had already been given. In those infinitesimal seconds the observations and calculations had been completed which were necessary to the solution of the problem of how, from a ship moving at thirty-one knots, to throw a quarter of a ton of steel and high explosive at another ship moving at twenty knots nine miles away.

'Shoot!' said the Gunnery Lieutenant loudly and still calmly, and then, as O'Flaherty pressed the trigger, he gave his next order. 'Up ladder, shoot!'

13

From the Captain's Report

. . . and hits were observed . . .

Chief Petty Officer Patrick O'Flaherty had been born a subject of the United Kingdom of Great Britain and Ireland, and for a short time he had been a subject of the Irish Free State before he enlisted in the British Navy and took the oath of allegiance to His Majesty the King of Great Britain and Northern Ireland. In the early days a few ill-mannered and stupid individuals among his shipmates had questioned him teasingly or casually as to the reason for his enlistment, but not one of them had asked him twice; even the stupidest could learn the lesson which O'Flaherty dealt out to them.

There had been wild times and black doings in Ireland in those days, and O'Flaherty as a child in his early teens had been through scenes of horror and blood; he may possibly have made enemies at that early age, although it is hard to imagine O'Flaherty even at fifteen being frightened of human enemies. One turn or another of Irish politics and of Irish guerrilla warfare may have resulted in O'Flaherty being deemed a traitor by his friends. In that fashion the boy may have found himself alone; or it may have been mere chance, some coincidence of raid and counter-raid that threw suspicion on him. There may have been no suspicion at all; the blood on O'Flaherty's hands may have called for the vengeance of someone too powerful or too cunning for the boy to oppose.

Perhaps, on the other hand, when peace descended upon Ireland, O'Flaherty may have joined the Navy out of mere desire for adventure, out of mere yearning for the sea that he knew in Clew Bay and Blacksod, possibly with the thought at the back of his mind that if he were ready to desert he would find in the British Navy endless opportunities of making a start in a fresh country without having to pay his fare thither.

But whatever was his motive, the British Navy had absorbed him. Its placid routine and its paternal discipline had been able to take a hold even on the wild Irish boy with the nerves of an unbroken colt. The kindly tolerance of the lower deck, where tolerance is the breath of life because there men have to live elbow to elbow for months together, won him over in the end – it cloyed him at first, sickened him at first, before he grew to understand it, and then to rely upon it. He came to love the breath of the sea, under equatorial stars in the Indian Ocean or freezing spray in the North Atlantic, as he had loved the soft air of Joyce's country. There had been black periods when the exile went through the uncontrollable misery of homesickness, but they had grown rarer with the years, as the boy of fifteen grew into the man of thirty-five, and providence, or good luck – or conceivably good management – had saved him during those times from breaches of discipline serious enough to ruin him.

Twenty years of service is a long time. Once he had

been a pink-cheeked boy, in the days when, ragged and hungry, he had been a thirteen-year-old soldier of Ireland, sleeping in the hills, hiding in the bogs, crouching behind a bank with half a dozen of his fellows waiting to pitch a bomb into a lorry-load of Black-and-Tans at the point where a bend in the road hid the felled tree. Now his cheeks were blue-black, and he was lantern-jawed; there were a few grey hairs among his wavy black ones, although the blue eyes under the black brows were as bright as ever, and the smile of the soft lips was as winning as ever. All the contradictions of Ireland were embodied in his person as in his career, just as obviously as they had been in the old days when the 'fighting blackguards' of Wellington's Connaught Rangers had stormed the castle of Badajoz in the teeth of the flailing musketry of Napoleon's garrison.

Today Chief Petty Officer O'Flaherty faced odds equally dreadful with his fighting blood as much aflame. His Irish sensitiveness and quickness of thought would not desert him, even when the Irish lust for battle consumed him – so that he reached by a different path the same exalted mental condition as the Gunnery Lieutenant who had entrusted him with his present duty. He kept the director sight upon the Italian flagship, holding it steady while the ship rolled, deeply to starboard, deeply to port, sighting for the base of the foremast and easing the director round millimetre by millimetre as *Artemis* head-reached upon the target ship. And with every microscopic variation of the director sight the six guns moved, too, along with their three turrets, five hundred tons of steel and machinery swaying to each featherweight touch upon the director, as miraculous as any wonder an Irish bard had ever sung about over his harp.

'Shoot!' said the Gunnery Lieutenant, loudly, and O'Flaherty pressed the trigger, completing the circuits in the six guns.

They bellowed aloud with their hideous voices, their deafening outcry tapering abruptly into the harsh murmur of the shells tearing through the air. And the shells were still on their way across the grey sea when the 'gun ready' lamps lit before the Gunnery Lieutenant's eyes.

'Shoot!' said the Gunnery Lieutenant.

O'Flaherty pressed the trigger again; the sights were still aligned upon the base of the Italian flagship's foremast.

'Shoot!' said the Gunnery Lieutenant, and again, 'Shoot!'

Twelve shells were in the air at once while the fountains raised by the six preceding ones still hung poised above the surface. This was the moment when heads must be utterly clear and hands utterly steady. Gunnery Lieutenant and Spotting Officer and Sub-Lieutenant Home forward in 'B' turret were watching those fountains, and pressing on the buttons before them to signal 'short' or 'straddle' or 'over'. Down in the Transmitting Station the signals from the three officers arrived together; if they were in agreement, or, if not, in accordance with the majority, the elevation of the guns was adjusted up or down the scale – the 'ladder' which the Gunnery Lieutenant had ordered – and to every round fired there were also added the innumerable other corrections: with an additional one now, because the guns were heating up. Yet every ten seconds the guns were ready and loaded, and every ten seconds the shells were hurled out of them, and the point where they fell, every ten seconds, had to be carefully noted – any confusion between one broadside and its predecessor or successor would ruin the subsequent shooting. The Gunnery Lieutenant could, when he wanted to, cut out completely the signals of the Spotting Officer and of 'B' turret officer, and rely entirely upon his own observations. But Raikes and Home were old and tried companions in arms. He could trust them – he stole a glance at Raikes' profile, composed and steady, and was confirmed in his decision. The Gunnery Lieutenant looked back quickly at the target. The next broadside raised a single splash this side of the target, and along the grey profile of the battleship a sparkling yellow flash, minute in the sunshine – another hit. Four hits with six broadsides was good shooting. That yellow flash was the consummation of a gunnery officer's career. It was for the sake of that that he endured the toil and drudgery of Whale Island, the endless drills, the constant inspection of apparatus; years of unremitting labour in order at the end of them to glimpse that yellow flash which told that the shells were hitting. The Gunnery Lieutenant stirred uneasily in his seat as within him surged the fighting spirit clamouring to hit and hit and go on hitting.

Now those bright flashes from the Italian flagship's sides were not hits. It was three seconds before the fall of another broadside was due. The Gunnery Lieutenant knew what they were. He spotted the fall of the next broadside and signalled it as 'short', and the fall of the next as 'straddle'. His finger was still on the button as the surface of the sea between him and the target rose in mountains, the incredible masses of water flung up by fifteen-inch shells.

'Shoot!' said the Gunnery Lieutenant.

With the bellow of the broadside sounded another tremendous noise, like that of a tube train hurtling through a tunnel – the sound of big shells passing close overhead. The Italian navy was firing back now. There were bright flashes all down the line; sea and air were flung into convulsions.

'Shoot!' said the Gunnery Lieutenant, and he marked up the next fall of shot.

And O'Flaherty at the director still kept the sights steady on the base of the Italian flagship's foremast, pressing the trigger as he was ordered, while the shells roared over him or burst in front of him and the guns thundered below him. That sensitive mouth of his – there was a girl in Southsea who still dreamed about that mouth occasionally – was smiling.

14

From the Captain's Report

. . . until I turned back again into the smoke screen . . .

On the bridge the sudden crash of the guns made Jerningham jump, the way it always did. He told himself that if he had any means of knowing just when that crash was coming he would not jump, but up here on the bridge there was no warning. He felt the hot blast of the explosion, and looked towards the enemy to see if he could spot the fall of the shot; so the crash of the next broadside caught him off his guard again and made him jump and miss it. He hoped none of the ratings on duty up here had seen him jump – that second time he was sure his feet had left the deck. The third crash came at that moment and he jumped again. The din was appalling, and with every broadside he was shaken by the blast of the guns.

He straightened his cap, which had fallen perilously lopsided: and tried to stiffen himself against the next broadside. It was hard to think in these conditions; those explosions jumbled a man's thoughts like shaking up a jigsaw puzzle. He felt envy, almost hatred, for the Officer of the Watch and the Torpedo Lieutenant and the Navigating Lieutenant standing together like a group of statuary. By the time he pulled himself together half a dozen broadsides had been fired; *Artemis* had been out of the smoke bank a full minute, Jerningham looked again to starboard in time to see the first Italian salvo fling up the sea before his eyes; then he heard another rumble terrifyingly close over his head. He saw the whole Italian line a-sparkle with gunfire. Every one of those ships was firing at him.

He gulped, and then with one last effort regained his self-control, panic fading out miraculously the way neuralgia sometimes did, and he was left savouring, almost doubtingly, his new-won calm, as, when the neuralgia had gone, he savoured doubtingly his freedom from pain. Remembering the notes he had to take regarding the course of the battle he took out pad and pencil again, referring to his wrist watch and making a hasty average of the time which had elapsed since his last entries and now. When he looked up again he saw the sea boiling with shell-splashes. It seemed incredible that *Artemis* could go through such a fire without being hit.

But the Captain was turning and giving an order to the Navigating Lieutenant, and then speaking into the voice pipe; the din was so terrific that Jerningham at his distance could hear nothing that he said. *Artemis* heeled and turned abruptly away from the enemy, and the gunfire ended with equal abruptness. Only a second or two elapsed before they were back again in the comforting smoke and darkness and silence; the smoke bank took the ship into its protection like a mother enfolding her child.

'God!' said Jerningham aloud, 'we're well out of that.'

He heard, but could not see, another salvo strike the

water close alongside; some of the spray which it threw up spattered on to the bridge. He wondered if the Italians were purposefully firing, blind, into the smoke, or if this was a salvo fired off by a shaken and untrained ship unable to check its guns' crews; as it became apparent that this was the only salvo fired it seemed that the second theory was the correct one.

The smoke was beginning to thin.

'Hard-a-starboard!' said the Captain, suddenly and a trifle more loudly than was his wont.

Artemis leaned steeply over, so steeply that the empty ammunition cases went cascading over the decks with a clatter that rang through the ship. The Navigating Lieutenant was saying the name of God as loudly as Jerningham had done, and was grabbing nervously at the compass before him. Jerningham looked forward. Dimly visible on the port bow were the upper works of a light cruiser, and right ahead was another, old *Hera*, the companion of *Artemis* in so many Mediterranean sallies. The ships were approaching each other at seventy miles an hour.

'Jesus!' said the Navigating Lieutenant, his face contorted with strain.

Jerningham saw *Hera* swing, felt *Artemis* swing. The two ships flashed past each other on opposite courses not twenty yards apart; Jerningham could see the officers on *Hera*'s bridge staring across at them, and the set faces of the ratings posted at *Hera*'s portside Oerlikon gun.

'Midships,' said the Captain. 'Steady!'

Artemis went back to a level keel, dashing along the windward edge of the smoke bank away from the rest of the squadron. The Navigating Lieutenant put two fingers into his collar and pulled against its constriction.

'That was a near thing, sir,' he said to the Captain; the calmness in his voice was artificial.

'Yes, pretty close,' replied the Captain simply.

It must have been very shortly after *Artemis* had turned into the smoke to attack the enemy that the Admiral had led the rest of the squadron back again on an opposite course, so that *Artemis* turning back through the smoke had only just missed collision with the last two ships in the line. But because of good seamanship and quick thinking no collision had taken place; that was the justification of the risk taken.

The Captain smiled, grimly and secretly, as he reconstructed the encounter in his mind. When ships dash about at thirty knots in a fogbank surprising things are likely to happen. A twenty-yard margin and a combined speed of sixty-two knots meant that he had given the order to starboard the helm with just half a second to spare. As a boy he had been trained, and as a man he had been training himself for twenty years, to make quick decisions in anticipation of moments just like that.

Back in 1918 the Captain had been a midshipman in the Grand Fleet, and he had been sent in his picket-boat with a message to the Fleet Flagship one day when they were lying at Rosyth. He had swung his boat neatly under *Queen Elizabeth*'s stern, turning at full speed, and then, going astern with his engines, had come to a perfect stop at the foot of *Queen Elizabeth*'s gangway. He had delivered his message and was about to leave again when a messenger stopped him.

'The Admiral would like to see you on the quarter-deck, sir.'

He went aft to where Acting-Admiral Sir David Beatty, GCB, commanding the Grand Fleet, was pacing the deck.

'Are you the wart who brought that picket-boat alongside?'

'Yes, sir.'

'Did you see my notice?'

'No, sir.'

'You've flooded my damned cabin with your damned wash. The first time the scuttles have been open for weeks. I go to the trouble of putting out a notice to say "slow" and the first damned little wart in his damned little picket-boat that comes alongside sends half the damned Firth of Forth over my damned furniture. My compliments to your Lieutenant, and you're to have six of the best. Of the *best*, remember.'

The midshipman displayed quickness of thought and firmness of decision to save himself from the pain and indignity of a beating. He stood his ground stubbornly.

'Well?' snapped the Admiral.

'That notice isn't hung so that anyone can see it coming under the ship's stern, sir. It's quite invisible from there.'

'Are you arguing with *me*?'

'Yes, sir. If the notice had been visible I should have seen it.'

That was a downright statement of fact, addressed boldly by a sixteen-year-old midshipman to the Commander-in-Chief. Beatty looked the boy up and down keenly, realizing that in this particular case a midshipman was sure of what he was saying. If his statement were to be put to the test it would probably prove to be correct; and to make the test would be a most undignified proceeding for an Admiral.

'Very good, then. I'll cancel my order. Instead you will report to your Lieutenant that you have been arguing with the Commander-in-Chief. I'll leave the verdict to him. Carry on.'

That was Beatty's quickness of decision. He could not be guilty of an act of injustice, but discipline might suffer if some unfledged midshipman would be able to boast of having bested him in an argument. He could rely on the Lieutenant to see to it that discipline did not suffer, to administer a beating for the purpose of making sure that the midshipman did not get too big for his boots. And in the end, the midshipman had escaped the beating by simply disobeying the Admiral's order. He had made no report to the Lieutenant, thereby imperilling his whole professional career and running the risk of dire punishment in addition; a big stake. But the odds were so heavy against the Commander-in-Chief inquiring as to whether a midshipman had made an obviously trivial report to his Lieutenant that it was a safe gamble which had succeeded.

In the mind of a boy of sixteen to argue with an Admiral and to disobey an order was as great a risk as it was for a captain to face the fire of the Italian navy and to charge through a smoke screen at thirty knots. There was risk in exposing a light cruiser to the fire of battleships. But, carefully calculated, the odds were not so great. *Artemis* emerged from the smoke screen ready to open fire. The Italians had to see her first, and then train their guns around, ascertain the range, open fire. Their instruments would not be as carefully looked after, nor as skilfully handled. It would take them much longer to get on to the target. And the more ships which fired upon *Artemis* the better; the numerous splashes would only serve to confuse the spotters and gunnery officers – a ship that tried to correct its guns' elevations by observing the fall of another ship's shells was lost indeed. The greatest risk to be run was that of pure chance, of a fluke salvo hitting the target, and against that risk must be balanced the utter necessity of hitting the Italians. The Captain had calculated the odds to a close approximation.

15

From the Captain's Report

. . . I then returned to continue the action . . .

'That was a near one,' said Leading Seaman Harris. He sat in the gunner's seat at the portside pompom and swung his legs as *Hera* tore past them. He grinned hugely, for Harris was of the graceless type that refuses to be impressed.

'Wonder 'ow old Corky's feeling,' said Able Seaman Ryder. 'D'you remember old Corky, Nibs? You know, the crusher. I 'eard 'e was in *'Era* now.'

A crusher is a member of the ship's police, and Ryder was a seaman familiar with those officials, like the majority of the pompom's crew. The ship's bad characters seemed to have gravitated naturally to the pompom. Leading Seaman Harris had been disrated more than once, and only held his responsible position because of a special endowment by nature, for Harris was a natural marksman with a pompom. To handle the gun accurately called for peculiar abilities – one hand controlling elevation and the other hand traversing the gun round, like playing the treble and the bass on a piano. And it had to be done instinctively, for there was no time to think when firing at an aeroplane moving at three hundred miles an hour. The complex four-barrelled gun, a couple of tons of elaborate machinery, had to be swung forward and back, up and down, not to keep on the target but to lead it by fifty yards or more so as to send its two-pound shells to rendezvous with the flying enemy. Even with a gun that fired four shells in a second, each with a muzzle velocity of unimaginable magnitude, and even with the help of tracer shells, it was a difficult task – the gunner had to be a natural shot and at the same time flexible enough of mind to submit to the necessary artificial restrictions of the training gear, lightning quick of hand and eye and mind – with the more vulgar attribute of plain courage so as to face unflurried the appalling attack of the dive bombers.

In *Artemis*, as in every ship, there was courage in plenty, but the ship had been combed unavailingly to find another pompom gunner as good as Leading Seaman Harris. He handled that gun of his as though it were a part of himself, looking along the sights with both eyes open, his unique mind leaping to conclusions where another would calculate. And experience had improved even Harris, because now he could out-think the bomber pilots and anticipate with equal intuition just what manoeuvres they would employ to throw off his aim. He was a virtuoso of the two-pounder pompom; this very morning he had increased his score by five – five shattered aeroplanes lay a hundred miles back at the bottom of the Mediterranean torn open by the shells Harris had fired into them.

So his crew were in higher spirits even than usual, like a successful football team after a match – it was a matter of teamwork, for the crew had to work in close coordination, supplying ammunition and clearing jams, like the half-backs making the openings for Harris the gifted centre-forward who shot the goals. Exultation rose high in their breasts, especially as the starboard side pompom could only claim one victim, and that doubtful. If the opportunity were to present itself before the exultation had a chance to die down the success would be celebrated in the way the gang celebrated every success, in indiscipline and lack of respect for superior officers – along with drunkenness and leave-breaking, these offences kept the port-side pompom crew under punishment with monotonous consistency.

'Convoy's copping it,' remarked Able Seaman Nye; a sudden burst of gunfire indicated that the convoy and its depleted escort were firing at the aeroplanes which had renewed the attack now that the cruisers, and destroyers, screen was out of the way.

'They won't come to no 'arm,' said Ryder. 'We got the cream of the Eyeties 'smorning.'

'Remember that one wiv the red stripes on 'is wings?' said Nibs. 'You got 'im properly, Leader.'

Harris nodded in happy reminiscence.

'How're you getting on, Curly?' he asked, suddenly.

Able Seaman Presteign smiled.

'All right,' he said.

Presteign was the right-handed loader of the pompom, his duty being to replace regularly the short heavy belts of shells on that side, a job he carried out accurately and unfailingly; that goes without saying, for if he had not he would never have remained entrusted with it, Harris's friendship notwithstanding. It was odd that he and Harris were such devoted friends. It was odd that Presteign was so quick and efficient at his work. For Presteign was a poet.

Not many people knew that. Jerningham did – one evening in the wardroom the Gunnery Lieutenant had tossed over to him one of the letters he was censoring, with a brief introduction.

'Here, Jerningham, you're a literary man. This ought to be in your line.'

Jerningham glanced over the sheet. It was a piece of verse, written in the typical uneducated scrawl of the lower deck, and Jerningham smiled pityingly as he first observed the shortness of the lines which revealed it to be lower-deck poetry. He nearly tossed it back again unread, for it went against the grain a little to laugh at someone's ineffective soul-stirrings. It was a little like laughing at a cripple; there are strange things to be read occasionally in the correspondence of six hundred men. But to oblige the Gunnery Lieutenant, Jerningham looked through the thing, reluctantly – he did not want to have to smile at crude rhymes and weak scansion. The rhymes were correct, he noted with surprise, and something in the sequence of them caught his notice so that he looked again. The verse was a sonnet in the Shakespearian form, perfectly correct, and for the first time he read it through with attention. It was a thing of beauty, of loveliness, exquisitely sweet, with a honeyed rhythm; as he read it the rhymes rang in his mental ear like the chiming of a distant church bell across a beautiful landscape. He looked up at the Gunnery Lieutenant.

'This is all right,' he said, with the misleading understatement of all the wardrooms of the British Navy. 'It's the real thing.'

The Gunnery Lieutenant smiled sceptically.

'Yes it is,' persisted Jerningham. He looked at the signature. 'Who's this A. B. Presteign?'

'Nobody special. Nice-looking kid. Curly, they call him. Came to us from *Excellent*.'

'Hostilities only?'

'No. Joined the Navy as a boy in 1938. Orphanage boy.'

'So that he's twenty now?'

'About that.'

Jerningham looked through the poem again, with the same intense pleasure. There was genius, not talent, here – genius at twenty. Unless – Jerningham went back through his mind in search of any earlier recollection of that sonnet. The man might easily have borrowed another man's work for his own. But Jerningham could not place it; he was sure that if ever it had been published it would be known to him.

'Who's it addressed to?'

'Oh, some girl or other.' The Gunnery Lieutenant picked out the envelope from the letters before him. 'Barmaid, I fancy.'

The envelope was addressed to Miss Jean Wardell, The Somerset Arms, Page Street, Gravesend; most likely a barmaid, as the Gunnery Lieutenant said.

'Well, let's have it back,' said the Gunnery Lieutenant. 'I can't spend all night over these dam' letters.'

There had been three other sonnets after that, each as lovely as the first, and each addressed to the same public house. Jerningham had wondered often about the unknown Keats on board *Artemis* and made a point of identifying him, but it was some time before he encountered him in person; it was not until much later that this happened, when they found themselves together on the pier waiting for the ship's boat with no one else present. Jerningham was a little drunk.

'I've seen some of your poetry, Presteign,' he said, 'it's pretty good.'

Presteign flushed slightly.

'Thank you, sir,' he said.

'What started you writing sonnets?' asked Jerningham.

'Well, sir –'

Presteign talked with a restrained fluency, handicapped by the fact that he was addressing an officer; also it was a subject he had never discussed before with anyone, never with anyone. He had read Shakespeare, borrowing the copy of the complete works from the ship's library; he gave Jerningham the impression of having revelled in Shakespeare during some weeks of debauch, like some other sailor on a drinking bout.

'And at the end of the book, sir –'

'There were the sonnets, of course.'

'Yes, sir. I never read anything like them before. They showed me something new.'

'"Then felt I like some watcher of the skies,"' quoted Jerningham, '"When a new planet swims into his ken."'

'Yes, sir,' said Presteign respectfully, but with no other reaction that Jerningham's sharp glance could observe.

'That's Keats. Do you know Keats?'

'No, sir.'

'Come to my cabin and I'll lend you a copy.'

There was something strangely dramatic about introducing Presteign to Keats. If ever there were two poets with everything in common, it was those two. In one way Jerningham regretted having made the introduction; he would have been interested to discover if Presteign would evolve for himself the classical sonnet form of octet and sextet. Presteign had undoubtedly been moving towards it already. But on the other hand there had been Presteign's enchanted enthusiasm over the 'Odes', his appreciation of the rich colour of 'The Eve of St Agnes'. There was something fantastically odd about the boy's beauty (there was no other word for it) in the strange setting of a sailor's uniform; his enthusiasm brought more colour to his cheeks and far more sparkle to his eyes. From the way his cropped fair hair curled over his head it was obvious how he came by his nickname.

And it was basically odd, too, to be talking about the 'Ode to a Nightingale' to a man whose duty it was to feed shells into a pompom, when England was fighting for her life and the world was in flames; and when Jerningham himself was in danger. Yet it was charming to listen to Presteign's intuitive yet subtle criticism of the Spenserian stanza as used by Keats in 'St Agnes'.

It was all intuitive, of course. The boy had never been educated; Jerningham ascertained the bald facts of his life partly from his own lips, partly from the ship's papers. He was a foundling (Jerningham guessed that his name of Presteign was given him after that of the Herefordshire village), a mere orphanage child. Institution life might have killed talent, but it could not kill genius; nothing could do that, not even the bleak routine, the ordered timetable, the wearisome drill, the uninspired food, the colourless life, the drab clothing, the poor teaching, the not-unkind guardianship. Sixteen years in an institution, and then the Navy, and then the war. The boy could not write an 'Ode to a Grecian Urn', he had never read an ode nor seen a Grecian urn. He had never heard a nightingale, and the stained glass in the institution chapel could never have suggested to him nor to Keats the rose-bloom falling on Madeline's hands.

He wrote about the beauties he knew of – the following gull; the blue and silver stern wave which curved so exquisitely above the stern of a fast-moving cruiser, as lovely as any Grecian urn; the ensign whipping stiffly from the staff; and he wrote about them in the vocabularies of the institution and the Navy, gaunt, exact words, transmuted by him into glowing jewels. Keats would have done the same, thought Jerningham, save that Milton and Byron had given him a freer choice.

And it is humanly possible that Navy discipline – Whale Island discipline – played its part in forming that disciplined poetic style. Jerningham formed the opinion that it had done so. That interested Jerningham enormously. Outwardly Presteign – save for his handsome face – was as typical a *matelot* as ever Jerningham had seen; if the institution had not taught him how to live in a crowded community the Navy certainly had done so. There was nothing of the rebel against society about Presteign; he had never come into conflict with rules and regulations – he wandered unharmed through them like a sleepwalker through bodily perils, carrying his supreme lyrical gift with him.

Yet in addition Jerningham came to realize that much of Presteign's immunity from trouble was due to his friendship with Harris – a strange friendship between the poet and the hard-headed sailor, but very real and intense for all that. Harris watched over and guarded Presteign like a big brother, and had done so ever since they first came into touch with each other at Whale Island – it was a fortunate chance that had transferred the pair of them simultaneously to *Artemis*. It was Harris who fought the battles for him that Presteign disdained to fight, and Harris who planned the breaches of the regulations that smoothed Presteign's path, and who did the necessary lying to save him from the consequences; Harris saw to it that Presteign's kit was complete and his hammock lashed up and stowed, reminded him of duties for which he had to report, and shielded him from the harsher contacts with his fellow men. Presteign's poetic gifts were something for Harris to wonder at, to admire without understanding; something which played no part in their friendship, something that Harris accepted unquestioning as part of his friend's make-up, on a par with the fact that his hair curled. And it may have been Presteign's exquisite sense of timing and rhythm which made him an efficient loader at the portside pompom, and that was the only return Harris wanted.

Up to the present moment Jerningham had only had three interviews with Presteign – not very long in which to gather all these facts about him, especially considering that he had spoilt the last interview rather badly.

'And who is Miss Jean Wardell?' asked Jerningham, as casually as he could – casually, but a sullen frown closed down over Presteign's sunny face when he heard the words.

'A girl I know,' he said, and then, as Jerningham looked further questions, 'a barmaid. In Gravesend.'

That sullenness told Jerningham much of what he wanted to know. He could picture the type, shopworn and a little overblown, uneducated and insensitive. Jerningham could picture the way a girl like that would receive Presteign's poems – the raised eyebrows, the puzzlement, the pretended interest for fear lest she should be suspected of a lack of culture. Now that they came by post they would be laid aside pettishly with no more than a glance – thrown away, probably. And Presteign knew all this about her, as that sullen glance of his disclosed; he was aware of her blowsiness and yet remained in thrall to her, the flesh warring with the spirit. The boy was probably doomed for the rest of his life to hopeless love for women older and more experienced than him – Jerningham saw that with crystal clearness at that very moment, at the same time as he realized that his rash question had, at least temporarily, upset the delicate relationship existing between officer and seaman, poet and patron. He had to postpone indefinitely the request he was going to put forward for a complete collection of Presteign's poetical works; and he had to terminate the interview as speedily as he decently could. After Presteign had left him he told himself again that poetry was something that did not matter, that a torpedo into a German submarine's side was worth more than all the sonnets in the world; and more bitterly he told himself that he would give all Presteign's poetry, written and to come, in exchange for a promise of personal immunity for himself during this war.

'How're you getting on, Curly?' asked Leading Seaman Harris, swinging his legs in the gunlayer's seat.

'All right,' said Presteign.

Something was forming in his mind; it was like the elaborate gold framework of a carefully designed and beautiful piece of jewellery, before the enamels and the gems are worked into it. It was the formula of a sonnet; the rhymes were grouping themselves together, with an overflow at the fifth line that would carry the sense on more vividly. That falling bomber, with the smoke pouring from it and the pilot dead at the controls, was the inspiration of that sonnet; Presteign could feel the poem forming itself, and knew it to be lovely. And farther back still in his mind there were other frameworks, other settings, constituting themselves, more shadowy as yet, and yet of a promise equally lovely. Presteign knew himself to be on the verge of a great outburst of poetry; a sequence of sonnets; the falling bomber, the Italian Navy ranged along the horizon, the Italian destroyer bursting into flames to split the night, the German submarine rising tortured to the surface; these were what he was going to write about. Presteign did not know whether ever before naval warfare had been made the subject of a sonnet-cycle, neither did he care. He was sure of himself with the perfect certainty of the artist as the words aligned themselves in his mind. The happiness of creation was upon him as he stood there beside the pompom with the wind flapping his clothes, and the stern wave curling gracefully behind the ship; grey water and white wake and blue sky; and the black smoke screen behind him. The chatter of his friends was faint in his ears as the first of the sonnet-cycle grew ever more and more definite in his mind.

''Ere we go again,' said Nibs.

Artemis was heeling over on the turn as she plunged back into the smoke screen to seek out her enemies once more.

16

From the Captain's Report
. . . further hits were observed until . . .

The smoke screen was only a little less dense this time; it was holding together marvellously well as that beautiful wind rolled it down upon the Italian line. The ventilating shafts took hold of the smoke and pumped it down into the interior of the ship, driving it along with the air into every compartment where men breathed. Acrid and oily at the same time, it dimmed the lights and it set men coughing and cursing. In 'B' turret, forward of the bridge and only just lower than it, the guns' crews stood by with the smoke eddying round them; their situation was better than that of most, because the ventilation here was speedier and more effective than in any other enclosed part of the ship. The guns were already loaded and they could feel the turret training round. Every man of the guns' crews had a skilled job to do, at some precise moment of the operation of loading and firing, and to keep a six-inch gun firing every ten seconds meant that each man must so concentrate on doing his work that he had no time to think of anything else; after a few minutes of action they would find it hard to say offhand on which side the turret was trained, and unless the loudspeaker or

Sub-Lieutenant Home told them they would know nothing about the damage their shots were doing. Their business was to get the guns loaded every ten seconds; the transmitting station would do their calculation for them, the director would point the guns and fire them. But they knew what the return into the smoke screen implied. It was hardly necessary for Sub-Lieutenant Home to tell them quietly.

'We shall be opening fire again in two minutes' time.'

Most of the men in 'B' turret were at least five years older than Home, and most of them, too, were still devotees of the beard-growing fashion which had swept the Royal Navy during the opening months of the war. There were black beards and fair beards and red beards in 'B' turret; the men could well have passed for a pirate crew instead of seamen of the Royal Navy. Most of them were dressed in soiled and ragged clothes, for, very sensibly, none of them saw any purpose in exposing their smart uniforms to damage in battle, especially as the majority of them spent a proportion of their pay in making their clothes smarter and better fitting than when issued by the Government.

A devotee of discipline of the old school would have been just as shocked to see the easy way in which they attended to their duties; a man did not spring to stiff attention when he had completed the operation for which he was responsible. He took himself out of the way of the others and stood poised to spring forward again. There was no need for the outward show of discipline, of the Prussian Guard type, with these men. They understood their business; they had worked those guns in half a dozen victories; they knew what they were fighting for; they were men of independent habit of thought working together with a common aim. They did not have to be broken into unthinking obedience to ensure that they would do what they were told; thanks to their victories and to the age-long victorious tradition of their service they could be sure that their efforts would be directly aimed towards victory.

It was true as well that every man knew that the better he did his work the better would be his chance of life, that for every Italian he helped to kill in this battle there was one less Italian who might kill him, but that was only a minor, a very minor reason for his doing his best. Love of life did not have nearly as much strength as did the love for the service which actuated these men, the love for the ship, and especially the artistic desire to do perfectly the task before them. They were in that way like the instrumentalists in an orchestra, playing their best and obedient to the conductor not through fear of dismissal but solely to produce a good performance. This state of mind of the men – this discipline and *esprit de corps* in other words, which would excite the hopeless envy of admirals not fortunate enough to command such men – made anything possible in the ship save cowardice and wilful inefficiency. The martyr at the stake refusing to recant to save his life, the artist unthinkingly putting his whole best into his work, were actuated by motives similar to those actuating these gunners – although anyone who rashly told those gunners that they were martyrs or artists would at best be answered only with the tolerance extended by the Navy towards an eccentric. They were masters of their craft, balancing easily on the heaving deck, ready for instant action although relaxed, the jokes which were passing among them having nothing to do with the situation in which they found themselves.

The ship passed out of the smoke screen; sunlight came in through the slits, and the smoke within began to dissipate under the forced ventilation. The deck under their feet took up a steep slant as *Artemis* turned; the pointer moved on the dial, and the turret rotated its heavy weight smoothly as Gunlayer Wayne kept his pointer following it. As the pointers coincided, with the guns loaded, the circuit was closed which illuminated the 'gun ready' lamp before the eyes of the Gunnery Lieutenant in the Gunnery Control Tower. And when Chief Petty Officer O'Flaherty pressed the trigger of the director, the little 'bridges' in the ignition tubes heated up, the tubes took fire, the detonators at their ends exploded into the cordite charges, the cordite exploded, and the guns went off in a smashing madness of sound, like a clap of thunder confined in a small room. The solid charges of cordite changed themselves into vast masses of heated gas, so much gas that if expanded at that temperature it would form a volume more than equal to that of the five-thousand-ton ship itself, but confined at the moment of firing into a bulk no bigger than a large loaf of bread under a pressure a hundred times as great as the heaviest pressure in any ship's boiler. The pressure thrust itself against the bases of the shells, forcing them up the twenty-five-feet guns, faster and faster and faster. The lands of the rifling took hold of the driving bands of the shells – that rifling was of the finest steel, for the pressure against the sides of the lands, as the shells inertly resisted rotation, was as powerful as that of a hydraulic press. Up the guns went the shells, faster and faster forward, and spinning faster and faster on their axes, until when they reached the muzzles twenty-five feet from the breech, they were rushing through the air at four times the speed of sound, having each acquired during that brief twenty-five feet an energy equal to that of a locomotive engine travelling at thirty miles an hour. And the recoil was exactly of the same amount of energy, as if each turret had been struck simultaneously by two locomotives moving at thirty miles an hour; but these two enormous blows fell merely on the recoiling systems of the guns – those recoiling systems over which so many ingenious brains had laboured, which represented the labour of so many skilled workmen, and which 'B' turret crew had kept in high condition through years of warfare. Unseen and unfelt, the hydraulic tubes of the recoil systems absorbed those two tremendous shocks; all that could be seen of their activity was the guns sliding slowly back and forward again. The two locomotives had been stopped in two seconds, as quietly as a woman might lean back against a cushion.

Number two at the right-hand gun was Leading Seaman Harley – the bearded seaman with the appearance of a benevolent Old Testament prophet; as the recoil ceased he opened the breech, and by that action sent a huge gust of compressed air tearing up the bore of the gun to sweep away the hot gases and any possible smouldering residue. He flicked out the old firing tube and pushed in a new one, closing the venthole. Numbers four and five were Seamen Cunliffe and Holt; they already had hold of the new shell, taken from the hoist, and they thrust it into the hot chamber of the gun. Cunliffe pushed with the rammer until the shell rested solidly against the rifling.

'Home!' shouted Cunliffe.

Able Seaman James was ready with the charge, and as Cunliffe withdrew the rammer James slid the charge into the breech and sprang back. Harley swung the breech shut, and the forward swing of the screw plug converted itself into a rotatory motion which interlocked the screw threads on breech and plug. As its motion stopped, Harley flicked over the interceptor which had up to that moment been guarding against accidents.

'Ready!' shouted Harley.

Wayne's pointer was exactly above the director pointer, and Harley had scarcely spoken when the guns crashed out anew, and the shells left the muzzles of the guns exactly ten seconds after their predecessors. Sub-Lieutenant Home looked through the glasses that were trained through the narrow slit under the roof of the turret. His gaze was fixed on the Italian flagship, but he was conscious, in the vague outer field of his vision, in the blue sky above the battleship, of a mysterious black line that rose and fell there, erasing itself at one end at the same time as it prolonged itself at the other. What he could see was the actual track of the shells winging their way through the air at two thousand feet a second; his position directly behind the guns gave him the advantage of following them with his glance as they rose three miles high and then descended again. The guns crashed out again below him, but he did not allow that to distract him, for he was looking for splashes. Just after this new explosion of the guns he saw the tiniest white chalk marks against the blue sky, appearing here and there behind the upper works of the battleship – hard to tell whether before or behind, but these had no visible roots, he was certain. Home snicked the 'over' button decisively, but this was no time to relax, for the next broadside was already on its way, writing its black line against the sky.

A single splash whose root he could see, white against the dark grey of the battleship; two more tiny white tips beyond, and a reddish-yellow gleam, at the base of the foremost funnel.

'Straddle,' muttered Home, marking it up.

He had to keep his head clear despite the din and the excitement. *Artemis* might have the most perfect instruments, the finest guns, the best ammunition ever made, but they were useless without clear heads and steady hands and keen eyes. It took a keen eye to see an 'over', so that it usually called for a bold decision to mark it up, and the three buttons were temptingly close to each other; a nervous man or a clumsy man or a shaken man could easily signal 'over' when he meant to signal 'short'. Home was only twenty years old; a mature man would smile at the idea of buying a house on Home's recommendation, or investing his money on Home's advice, or even backing a horse that Home might fancy. The women who might meet him in drawing-rooms or at cocktail parties would think of him – if they thought of him at all – as a 'nice boy'; even the girls younger than him would hardly bother their heads about a penniless sub-lieutenant – someone they could dance with, a convenient escort on an otherwise empty evening, perhaps, but not someone to be taken seriously. Moreover, Sub-Lieutenant Home was not a young man with social graces, and he had an inborn tendency to mild stupidity; hostesses found him heavy in the hand.

He was not a man of active and ingenious mind, and people who knew him well would predict for him only the most undistinguished future – retirement from the Navy in twenty years or so with the rank of Lieutenant-Commander, presumably. It might in consequence be considered strange to find him in such a responsible position as captain of 'B' turret, but there was really nothing strange about it. Home was a man with all the dogged courage of the society whence he came. He could be relied upon to die where he stood – where he sat, rather – sooner than desert his post. His quiet unimaginative mind was unmoved by fear or by fear of responsibility; as he pressed those buttons he did not dwell mentally on the consequences of pressing the wrong one – the broadside that might miss, the defeat that might ensue from that, the fall of Malta as a consequence of the defeat, the loss of Egypt as a result of the fall of Malta, the victory of Germany, the enslavement of the world. Home may have been worried a little at the thought of a 'ticking-off' from the Gunnery Lieutenant, but beyond that his imagination did not stray. He merely made sure that he pressed the right button and observed the fall of the successive broadsides in their proper sequence. He would go on doing that until the end of time; and if evil fortune should wipe out the Gunnery Control Tower and the Gunnery

Lieutenant he was perfectly prepared to take over the direction of the three turrets from where he sat and carry the responsibility of the whole ship's armament.

The bearded ruffians who manned 'B' turret accorded him the respect due to his rank and the devotion they were ready to give anyone who could be relied upon come what might to direct their endeavours to destroy the Eyeties. They knew him well after all these months of service, could predict with complete certainty what would be his attitude towards any of the usual crimes or requests. Even though he still only had to shave alternate days while their beards had grey hairs in them, he wore a gold stripe on his sleeve and he could (with discreet aid from tables) work out problems in ballistics or navigation which they never had any hope of solving – the two attributes were very much on a par with each other in their estimation; in other words they knew him to be a major cog in the complex machine in which they were minor cogs, but they also knew that the major cog would never break under the strain or jam through some unpredictable flaw.

17

From the Captain's Report
. . . a hit started a small fire . . .

Artemis was shooting superbly. The Captain could see that, with his own eyes, as he turned his binoculars upon the Italian flagship. With the shortened range it was possible to see not merely whether the splashes fell this side or the other of the target, but how close they fell, and they were raining so densely round the battleship that there must be many more hits being scored than were revealed by the fleeting gleams of the bursting shells which he could see; others were being obscured by the splashes or were bursting inside plating. It was impossible that they could do any serious damage to the big battleship with her vitals encased in twelve-inch steel, but they must be discommoding, all the same. The Captain experienced a feeling of elation which was extraordinarily pleasant. He was a man who was profoundly interested in the art of living. Rembrandt gave him pleasure, and so did the Fifth Symphony; so did bouillabaisse at Marseilles or southern cooking at New Orleans or a properly served Yorkshire pudding in the north of England; so did a pretty girl or an elegant woman; so did a successful winning hazard from a difficult position at billiards, or a Vienna coup at bridge;

and so did success in battle. These were the things that gilded the bitter pill of life which everyone had to swallow. They were as important as life and death; not because they were very important, but because life and death were not very important. So the Captain allowed himself to enjoy both the spectacle of shells raining down upon the Italian flagship, and the knowledge that it was his own achievement that they should rain down like that.

The enemy's salvoes were creeping closer; it was nearly time to retire again. A mile away *Hera* had emerged from the smoke screen, spitting fire from all her turrets. It seemed for a moment as if she were on fire herself, for during her passage through the smoke screen she had breathed the smoke in through her ventilators, and now her forced ventilation system was blowing it out again in wreathes that curled round her superstructure so that she looked like a ghost ship. *Artemis* must have presented the same appearance when she came through the screen; the Captain was a little annoyed with himself for not having thought of it and borne it in mind – it would be of some importance in hampering the Italian rangefinders and gunlayers.

But with *Hera* out of the screen, and the other cruisers beginning to show beyond her, it was for *Artemis* to withdraw and leave the Italians to their weary task of getting the range of these new elusive targets. It would be ideal if the English ships were only to show themselves for so long that the Italians had no chance of firing on them at all, but that was a council of perfection, and impractical; what was to be aimed at was to strike an exact balance between rashness and timidity, to stay out as long as possible so as to do the most damage and yet not to run undue risks from the enemy's fire.

'Port ten,' said the Captain, waiting until a broadside did not drown his voice, and *Artemis* plunged back into the protecting smoke.

'Gawd!' said Leading Seaman Harris down at the portside pompom, 'back in the smoke again! Slow, I call it.'

Not many of the ship's company of *Artemis* would have called her proceedings slow, but Harris had something of the spoilt prima donna about him. He wanted to be in action with his gun against dive bombers, and he faintly resented the main battery of the ship having a turn at all.

'It's this blasted smoke I can't stand,' grumbled Nibs. 'It makes me feel filthy under my clothes.'

An Italian salvo rumbled overhead and plunged unseen into the sea beyond.

'Wouldn't call it slow meself,' said Ryder.

'Where's Curly?' asked Harris. 'You all right, Curly?'

'Yes,' said Presteign. He was all right. The sonnet on the falling bomber, plummetting in flames into the sea, was nearly fully shaped in his mind, and he knew it to be good. 'I'm all right, Leader.'

Then it happened. No one can explain it. Fifty salvoes had been fired at *Artemis* without scoring a hit, and now, when she was invisible in the fog, a chance shell hit her. It struck full on the portside pompom, smashing it into jagged splinters of steel as swift as rifle bullets, plunged on and down, through the deck, and there it burst. On the edge of the huge crater it opened in the deck lay what was left of Presteign and Harris, and their blood mingled in the scuppers, so that in their deaths they were joined together.

Artemis staggered under the blow. In the engine-room, in the turrets, on the bridge, men grabbed for handhold to preserve their footing. That shell had struck *Artemis* with the force of an express train travelling at sixty miles an hour, with nothing to cushion the shock, nothing to resist it save the frail plating. But a trifle had saved her from utter destruction; the fact that in its plunging course the shell had struck the heavy pompom, five feet above the deck. The gun had been smashed into unrecognizable fragments by the blow, all its tons of steel torn into splinters, but on the other hand the fuse of the shell had been started into action. The ingenuity of man has progressed so far that as well as being able to throw a shell weighing a ton at a speed of two thousand feet a second, he can divide that second into thousandths, and arrange for the shell to explode either on impact or one two-hundredth of a second later, when it might be expected to be inside any armour plate it might strike. Having struck the pompom, the shell burst only just beneath the upper deck; had it not done so, it would have burst below the main deck, and it would have torn *Artemis* in two.

What it did was bad enough. It tore open a huge crater in the deck – a vast hole ringed round with a rough edge – long jagged blades of steel, blown vertical by the explosion. It tore huge holes in the ship's side, and drove red-hot fragments here, there and everywhere, forward through the frail bulkheads, down through the main deck, aft through the plating into the handing-room of 'X' turret. The mere force of its impact, the conversion of its energy of motion into heat, was sufficient to make steel white hot, and within the shell were hundreds of pounds of high explosive which turned the middle of the ship into a raging furnace. Below the upper deck, at the point where the shell burst, was the wardroom, where were the Surgeon Lieutenant-Commander and his men, and two casualties hit by bomb splinters earlier in the morning. One moment they were alive, and the next they were dead, one moment they were men, and then the shell burst right in their midst, and they were nothing – nothing.

The heat of the explosion was like the heat of an oxy-acetylene flame, like the heat of an electric furnace. The paint on the bulkheads of the wardroom was only the thinnest possible layer – kept thin with this particular emergency in view – but it burst into raging flames, as if the very plating had caught fire. The scant covering of linoleum on the deck burst into flames. The padding of the chairs caught fire. The bulkhead forward, dividing the wardroom from its stores, had been torn open, and the stores caught fire, all the sparse pitiful little things which brought some amenity into the lives of the officers: tablecloths and table-napkins, newspapers and spirits, the very bread and sugar, all blazed together. On the starboard side of the ship beside the wardroom were the senior officers' cabins. They blazed as well – bedding and desks and clothing, paint and woodwork, and photographs of their wives and children, hockey sticks and tennis rackets. From side to side of the ship, from 'X' turret aft beyond the warrant officers' mess forward, the ship was a raging furnace, with flames and smoke pouring out of her riddled hull. Cascading into the flames fell the ammunition of the shattered pompom – deadly little shells, bursting in a devil's tattoo of explosions and feeding the flames which blazed luridly in the gloom of the smoke screen.

The Commander – Commander James Hipkin Rhodes, DSO, DSC – had been squatting on the boat deck aft, complaining bitterly to himself. When he had been a young lieutenant it had appeared such an unattainable apothesis to become a Commander even when he attained the unattainable and won the vital promotion – the most difficult and most significant in a naval officer's career – from lieutenant-commander to commander it had been delightful and gratifying. But to be Commander in a light cruiser in action was to be a fifth wheel to a coach: it meant squatting here on the boat deck doing nothing at all, waiting merely for unpleasantness – waiting in case the Captain should be killed (and the Commander would rather be killed himself, with no sort of pose about that option) and waiting for the ship to be hit (and the Commander loved *Artemis* more dearly than most men love their wives).

On active service it was hard enough to keep the ship at all clean and presentable, the way any self-respecting commander would have his ship appear. He groaned each time *Artemis* dashed into the smoke screen – he knew too well the effect that oily vapour would have on paint and bedding and clothing. A commander's duty in a big ship is largely one of routine, and after two years of that duty it can be understood that Rhodes had become too deeply involved in it, was liable to think too much about details and not about the broad outline of the fact that England was fighting for her life. As *Artemis* went into action he had been wondering what damage would be done to his precious paint, just as a woman's first reaction when she and her husband receive an invitation to some important function might be to wonder what she should wear. Rhodes, in fact, was in grave danger of becoming an old woman.

The shell burst, and the blast of the explosion flung him from his seat sprawling on the deck. His chin was lacerated, and when he got to his feet blood poured down his chest, but he paid no attention to it. He staggered to the rail, sick and shaken, and gazed down at the ruin six feet below him. The heat of the flames scorched his face. Then he rallied.

'Hoses, there!' he bellowed; the crew of the starboard side pompom – those who had not been mown down by the splinters – were picking themselves up out of the fantastic attitudes into which they had been flung, and the light of the flames lit them vaguely in the artificial darkness of the smoke. The voice of an officer pulled them together. Without knowing what they did they got out the hoses, going like automatons through the drill that had been grained into them. *Artemis* came out of the smoke screen, and the flames paled almost into invisibility against the sunshine, masked by the thick grey smoke pouring up through the deck – foul, stinking smoke, for many things were burning there.

Rhodes half fell, half ran down the ladder to the upper deck, calling together the fire-fighting parties in the waist. The pumps began to sing; the prescience of the Commander (E) had provided ample steam for them. Rhodes plunged down to the mess flat below; it was full of smoke both from the screen and from the fire, and pitchy-black with the failure of the electric circuits – so dark that he could see, as he looked aft, the afterbulkhead glowing lurid red with the heat beyond it.

Rhodes was an old woman no longer. The explosion of a fifteen-inch shell had been sufficient to shake him at least temporarily out of his old-womanishness. He organized the fire-fighting arrangements here, and then dashed up again to the boat deck where he could have the clearest view of the damage. There was no way of getting aft from here direct – the ship was ablaze from side to side – and the only way left would be to go down into the boiler-room and aft from there, under the fire. That would take a long time. He caught sight of Richards on the quarterdeck; he was in charge of damage control in the after part of the ship, and as Richards was alive and had a working party with him there was no urgent need for Rhodes's presence. He turned to the telephone.

'Forebridge,' he said, and then when Jerningham answered, 'Commander to Captain.'

The two brief waits, of a second or two each time, gave him time to get his breath and steady himself. For Rhodes there was some advantage about being old-maidish and fussy about detail. Being deeply immersed in his job shut out other considerations from his mind. He had to make a formal report, and it had to be done exactly right.

'Yes, Commander?' said the Captain's voice.

Rhodes reported what he had seen and done.

'Is it a bad fire?' asked the Captain.

The Commander let his eyes roam back aft, to the smoke and flame. From a commander's point of view it was a very bad fire indeed, but Rhodes still had some common sense left to save him from exaggeration. He made himself look at the flames with a dispassionate eye, the eye of a fighting man and not that of the ship's head housemaid.

'No, sir,' he said. 'Not a bad fire. It'll be under control directly.'

He put back the receiver and the instrument squealed at once so that he took it up again. The damage reports were coming in from the different compartments – a small leak here, a shattered bulkhead there. Nothing to call for a serious transference of his damage-control strength. Jerningham showed up beside him, a little white about the gills, but his manner was quite composed. Jerningham and the Commander disliked each other for a variety of reasons, and there was no pretence of cordiality as they spoke to each other. The Commander hastily recapitulated the reports which had come in to him, and Jerningham made notes on his pad, before they turned back to look at the fire.

A score of hoses were pouring water into the flaming crater; one or two pompom shells were still exploding down below, each explosion sending up a torrent of sparks like some vast firework. Another hose party came running down the waist on the portside; the man who held the nozzle dragged Presteign's dead body viciously out of the way. The jets would have mastered the fire soon enough, but a more powerful agency came into play. *Artemis* put her helm over, and as she heeled the hole torn in her side was brought below the surface, and the sea rushed in. Even on the upper deck they could hear the crackling as the water quenched the red-hot surfaces, and steam poured in a huge cloud up through the crater, enwreathing the whole stern of the ship. Then she righted herself as she took up her new course, then leaned a little the other way as the rudder steadied her, sending fifty tons of water washing through the compartment into every corner and cranny before it poured down in sooty warm shower-baths through the few holes torn in the main deck by the shell fragments. Only a little steam and smoke came up through the deck now; Richards stood on the jagged edge of the crater and looked down, while a petty officer beside him jumped down into the wrecked wardroom amid the unspeakable mess inside. Richards with his hands to his mouth bellowed the result of his inspection to the Commander – the holes in both sides of the ship above the water line, the minor holes in the deck.

'I'll get those holes patched in a jiffy,' said the Commander to Jerningham. 'Report that to the Captain.'

'Aye aye, sir,' said Jerningham, remembering the need to salute only in the nick of time as he turned away.

The Commander promptly forgot Jerningham in the happier business of organizing. He was calling up in his mind where he had stored the rubber slabs, the battens and timbers that he would need for patching the holes, the ratings whom he would detail for the work. He had in his mind a clear picture of the things he had to do and the order in which he would do them as he ran down to the upper deck and set about the work, while Jerningham made his way back from the boat deck to the bridge and delivered his message to the Captain.

It had been rank bad luck that *Artemis* had been hit at all, but on the other hand the bad luck was balanced by the good luck that dictated how little damage had been done. A shell in the wardroom, with only the most minor damage below the main deck, would do the ship less harm practically than if it had burst in any other spot. No damage had been done to the ship's main armament, and the casualty list was small. The wardroom flat would flood and flood again as *Artemis* manoeuvred, before the Commander could get his patches into place, but (the Captain worked out the problem roughly in his head) her stability would not be greatly endangered by the weight of that mass of water above the water line. She had plenty of reserve to deal with that, despite the shifting of weights as a result of firing off thirty tons of shells. A pity about the Surgeon Lieutenant-Commander and his men.

'The port-side pompom's crew's wiped out, you say?' said the Captain.

'Yes, sir.'

'Then Harris has gone.'

'Yes, sir.'

So *Artemis* had lost her phenomenal pompom gunner. Probably he was irreplaceable – the ship would never see his like again.

Jerningham thought of Presteign. He knew – he felt in his bones – that the Gravesend barmaid had crumpled up and thrown away each of those sonnets as they had reached her. And he had never got from Presteign that complete copy of his work. Something had been lost to civilization. Jerningham had been shaken by the explosion into a numbed state of mind; that part of him which had been trained into a naval officer was functioning only dully and semi-automatically, and it was strange that the other part of him should have this piercing insight and feel this bitter sense of loss. He would tell the Captain about Presteign some day if they ever came out of this battle alive.

Four destroyers were racing alongside of *Artemis*, overhauling her as they dashed to head off the Italian line. Signal flags went fluttering to the masthead of the leader, and the Chief Yeoman of Signals began to bellow his interpretation of them.

18

From the Captain's Report

. . . without serious damage . . .

The ship's company of *Artemis* knew the Torpedo Gunner's Mate to be a misanthrope – they had suffered for long under his misanthropy – and it may have been that which led the lower deck to believe him to be a bigamist. Certainly the most circumstantial stories were told about the Torpedo Gunner's Mate's matrimonial affairs, of the grim wife he had in Pompey, a wife apparently as repellent as himself, and of the charming young girl he was reputed to be bigamously married to in Winchester. Some went as far as to say that this new wife was his first wife's niece, or some blood relation at least, and there was always much speculation about the occult power by which he had contrived to win her affection and induce her to be an accessory in that particular crime of all crimes. He was an old man, too, as sailors count age, called back into service after retiring on pension, and the wags would raise a laugh sometimes by wondering what Nelson had said to the Torpedo Gunner's Mate when they last met.

Whatever might be the Torpedo Gunner's Mate's matrimonial vagaries on shore, at sea he was a single-minded man, a man with only one interest, which probably accounted for the ship's company's jests – a single-minded man is a natural butt. He was engrossed, to the exclusion of all other interests, in the ship's electricity supply and distribution. All his waking thoughts and most of his dreams dealt with electricity, as a miser can only think of his hoard. According to the Torpedo Gunner's Mate, no one else in the ship knew anything worth knowing about electricity; the Torpedo Lieutenant might be able to work out the text-book problems about inductance and hysteresis, but that sort of theoretical nonsense was of no use to a man confronted with the necessity of supplying electricity to every nook and cranny of a ship in every condition. The Torpedo Lieutenant certainly could not shut his eyes and count slowly along the main port-side distributing main, ticking off one by one every branch, every fuse-box, and every switch, but the Torpedo Gunner's Mate could do that, and he could do the same for the accessory port-side distributing main, and then pass over to the starboard side and do it all over again.

The Torpedo Gunner's Mate had the loftiest contempt for anyone who could not do that, which meant that he had the loftiest contempt for everyone in the ship. And because nothing in the ship could operate properly without electricity everybody on board, the Captain, the Commander, whose word was law, the Commander (E), the Torpedo Lieutenant, the Gunnery Lieutenant whose guns' crews considered themselves the most important people in the ship, every man Jack of them, in the Torpedo Gunner's Mate's mind, was a mere puppet dependent upon him for everything beyond the mere breath of life – and, considering the number of electrically operated fans, they were dependent on him for that as well. He knew, even although no one else knew it, that he was lord and master of HMS *Artemis*; that by opening or closing a few switches he could cut the thread of her life just as the Greek Fates cut the thread of the lives of mankind. He hugged that knowledge to himself secretly, as passionately as he hugged to his bosom the fair-haired charmer of Winchester. It was a constant source of secret gratification to him, not realizing in his blindness that at the same time the power was quite useless to him in consequence of his fixed determination to keep the electricity supply of *Artemis* functioning perfectly – he could no more have flouted that determination than he could have cut off his own nose.

The Torpedo Gunner's Mate's action station was beside the great switchboard, deep down in the bowels of the ship, and that was the place where he would rather be than anywhere else in the world – with the occasional exception of Winchester. He could feast his eyes on the dials and the indicator lights, run them once more over the huge wiring diagram, enjoying every moment of it – like a miser with his hoard again, fingering the coins and adding up the totals for the thousandth time with as much pleasure as the first. He took a glance at the specific gravity of the acid in the storage batteries; there was enough electricity there to fill the demands of the whole ship for three hours if necessary should the generators be damaged, and in three hours either the poor fools could get the generators working again or the damage must be such that the ship was lost. He was checking over the switchboard again when the shell struck and burst, and the deck beneath his feet heaved and flung him crashing down. He was on his feet again directly, disentangling himself from the rating who was stationed there with him to take his place if he became a casualty – as if the miserable ignoramus could possibly take his place! – and turned his eyes at once to the switchboard, to the dials and the indicator lamps. His assistant got to his feet beside him, but the Torpedo Gunner's Mate jealously elbowed him back; no man while he was on duty would touch that switchboard except himself.

Some of the lamps were out; some of the needles on the dials were back to zero. The Torpedo Gunner's Mate ran his hands over the switches like a pianist trying out a piano. He played a scale on them, switched over to the alternative main, and played the scale again, never having to take his eyes from the indicators as he did so – he could lay his hands blindfolded on any switch he chose. The lighting circuit to the after-mess flat was broken, and the Torpedo Gunner's Mate restored it; he did the same for other parts of the ship, for all except the wardroom flat. The indicator here remained obstinate. Nothing he could do could restore the flow of electricity in the wardroom flat. As far as the Torpedo Gunner's Mate was concerned, the wardroom flat had ceased to exist. He grunted as he reached this conclusion; not even his assistant, who was looking now at him instead of at the board, and who had borne with his moods for two and a half years, could tell what that grunt meant, or could interpret the stony expression in his face.

The Torpedo Gunner's Mate grunted again, and let

his hand fall from the switchboard. He walked forward, rolling a trifle stiffly with the motion of the ship – he was a little troubled with rheumatism in the knees – and passed through the door into the telephone exchange. Here he surveyed the scene with a jealous eye, for only very partially was the telephone exchange under his charge. He supplied it with electricity, but Seamen Howlett and Grant who manned the telephone switchboard were not under the orders of his department, and the Torpedo Gunner's Mate strongly believed that they would be more efficient if they were. He did not like the fact that men who dispensed electricity – even in the minute quantities necessary to actuate a telephone receiver – should not be under his supervision, and the work they were doing now, of testing the circuits and ascertaining which ones were still functioning, was so like the duty he had just completed as to rouse his jealousy still further.

He watched their deft motions for a brief space – he knew as much about their duty as they did themselves – and ran his eye over the telephone switchboard to check what they were doing. Here and there the board was spanned criss-cross by wires plugged in for the duration of the action, completing circuits which enabled the Gunnery Lieutenant to speak at will with his turrets and magazines, the boiler-room with the engine-room, and so on. The Torpedo Gunner's Mate was a little disappointed to see that the permanent circuits were correct; he could tell by the set of their shoulders that Howlett and Grant, despite the earphones on their ears and their preoccupation with their duty, were aware of his entrance and of the fact that he was brooding over them.

A light glowed on the switchboard and Howlett plugged in.

'Exchange,' he said.

The Torpedo Gunner's Mate could not hear the murmur in Howlett's earphone, but he saw where he plugged in the connection. Forebridge wanted to speak with sick bay – nothing very remarkable about that.

'One of you lads get me the Damage Control Officer,' said the Torpedo Gunner's Mate, picking up the telephone receiver beside him. 'This is a priority call.'

That was a gratifying thing to be able to say; during his brief watch over the switchboard he had been able to see how much in demand was the Damage Control Officer's telephone, and the fact that he could claim priority and insist on his own call being put through next, was a most satisfactory tribute to the importance of electricity. He heard the Commander's voice, and proceeded to report the result of his tests at the main switchboard.

'Very good,' said the Commander. 'Yes. Yes, the wardroom flat's been burnt out.'

The Torpedo Gunner's Mate put back the receiver and eyed again for a moment the unresponsive backs of Howlett and Grant. He was jealous of these two. They could listen to the telephone conversations, and even if they were too busy to do that they could still guess, from the origins and destinations of the calls coming through, what was going on in the ship. They shared his knowledge about the wardroom flat, and it was not fair – it was actually indecent – that it should be so. What he knew and ought to know by virtue of his position as dispenser of electricity they knew because they could take advantage of the duty to which they happened to be assigned. It was not consistent with the dignity of the Torpedo Gunner's Mate, in charge of the main switchboard – no, much more than that, it was not consistent with the dignity of electricity itself – that he should not be solitary on a pinnacle of exclusive knowledge. He saw Howlett dart a glance at Grant, and he read amusement in it, something almost approaching insolence; what mollified the Torpedo Gunner's Mate and distracted him from taking instant action in defence of his dignity was the sight of the left side of Grant's face – so far he had seen only the back of Grant's head. Grant's left eye was blackened and puffy, the lids swollen and gorged. There was a contusion on his cheekbone which would probably turn black as well, and the cheek itself showed a faint bruise which reappeared lower down over the jawbone in more marked fashion.

'That's a rare shiner you've got there, Grant,' said the Torpedo Gunner's Mate.

'It is an' all,' said Grant, who despite his name, was born and bred in Manchester. Another light glowed on the switchboard, and Grant plugged in. 'Exchange.'

The explosion of the shell must have lifted Grant up from his chair and dashed him, face foremost, against the switchboard.

'Exchange,' said Grant and Howlett simultaneously, plugging in.

It was a trifle of a pill for the Torpedo Gunner's Mate to swallow for him to acknowledge to himself that the telephone switchboard was being properly looked after without his supervision, that these children of twenty or so would do their duty whether he kept his eye on them or not. The Torpedo Gunner's Mate had little faith in the young. He sighed and turned away, walking out of the telephone room back to his own treasured switchboard; his rheumatism gave him an old man's gait. He ran his eye over the dials and indicator lights; all was still well here; even his fool of an assistant rating had not managed to do anything wrong. The Torpedo Gunner's Mate continued to walk aft, through another door and into the most secret part of the ship.

He closed the door behind him and looked round. This was the Transmitting Station; the Torpedo Gunner's Mate knew that any foreign power, even in time of peace, would pay a King's ransom for the chance of having one of their experts stand for half an hour where he stood now. All about him were the superhuman machines upon which the best brains of the Navy had laboured for years in search of perfection, the machines which solved instantaneously the differential equations which would occupy a skilled mathematician for a couple of days or more, the machines which correlated half a dozen different sets of data at once, the machines which allowed for barometric pressure and for gun temperatures, machines that looked into the future and yet never forgot the past.

It was comforting to the Torpedo Gunner's Mate to know that these superhuman things were dependent on him for the supply of electricity which alone allowed them to function; the only crony he had in the ship, Chief Electrical Artificer Sands (another man with proper ideas regarding the importance of electricity), spent most of his waking hours adjusting them and tuning them, pandering to their weaknesses and being patient with them when they turned obstinate.

In the centre of the room, ranged round a table large enough for a Lord Mayor's banquet to be served on it, sat the Marine band. In the old days travelling theatrical companies expected their players to do a double job, and take their places nightly in the orchestra preliminary to appearing on the stage; there would be advertisements in the theatrical papers for a 'heavy' who could 'double in brass'. Similarly, in *Artemis*, the musicians had a double duty, and the provision of music was the less important. The time they spent rehearsing 'Colonel Bogey' and 'A Life on the Ocean Wave' was only the time that could be spared from rehearsals of a more exacting piece of teamwork. The machines all round them, the superhuman machines, even when the Torpedo Gunner's Mate had supplied them with electricity and Chief Electrical Artificer Sands had tuned them to perfection, were still dependent upon human agency to interpret and implement their findings. Under the glass top of the table there were needles which moved steadily and needles which moved erratically, needles which crept and needles which jumped, and each needle was watched by a bandsman who had his own individual pointer under his control which had to keep pace with it, creep when it crept, jump when it jumped, utterly unpredictably. At the Transmitting Station table every item the Marine band played was unrehearsed and without score; the instrumentalists could never look ahead and find that some individuals among them had been allotted twenty bars' rest by the composer. There was no looking ahead, and each bandsman was obeying a different baton which might at any moment leap into activity and summon him to action.

At the head of the table, sitting on a higher chair which gave him a view over the whole expanse, sat the Commissioned Gunner, Mr Kaile, his telephone instrument clasped over his head, the other telephones within reach. In one sense, Mr Kaile was conductor of this mad hatter's orchestra. He had no control over what air should be played, nor when it should begin or end. He was rather in the position of a band leader who may find his instrumentalists suddenly striking up together at any moment without agreeing on the tune. He had to see that at least every instrument was in the same key and kept the same time, and, in accordance with the orders that came down from the bridge and from the Gunnery Lieutenant, and guided by the triple reports of the spotting officers, he was also expected – to continue the analogy – to swell or diminish the volume of sound as might be considered necessary; in other words, to send the range up or down the ladder, deflect to right or to left, as the direct observation of the fall of the shells might dictate.

However perfect the machines, war in the last analysis is fought by men whose nerves must remain steady to direct the machines, whose courage must remain high when they, as well as their machines, are in danger; whose discipline and training must be such that they work together. Every improvement in the machines does not dispose of this problem, but only pushes it one remove farther along. The Paleolithic man who first thought of setting his flint axe in a haft instead of holding it clumsily in his hand still had to face and fight his enemy. Nelson's gunners had their ammunition brought to them by powder monkeys instead of by an automatic hydraulic hoist like the gunners in *Artemis*, but in either case the gunners had to stand by their guns to achieve anything.

So similarly round the table of the Transmitting Station it was necessary that there should be discipline and courage. Trembling hands could not keep those pointers steady, nor could minds distracted by fear be alert to follow the aimless wanderings of the guiding needles so that the guns above could continue to hurl forth their broadsides every ten seconds. Down here, far below the level of the sea, the men were comparatively protected from shell fire, but not far below their feet was the outer skin of the ship, and around them were the bunkers of oil fuel. Mine or torpedo might strike there, engulfing them in flame or water. Other compartments of the ship might be holed, and the sea pour in as the ship sank slowly; in that case it would be their duty to remain at their posts to keep the guns firing to the last, while above them there were only the difficult iron ladders up which they might eventually climb to precarious life.

The Marine bandsmen were perfectly aware of all this – they were far too intelligent not to be. It was discipline which kept them at the table; it was even discipline which kept their hands steady and their heads clear. Intangible and indefinable, discipline might perhaps be more clearly understood by consideration of one of its opposites. Panic can seize a crowd or an individual, making men run for no known reason in search of no known objective; in panic men shake with fear, act without aim or purpose, hear nothing, see nothing. Disciplined men stay calm and steady, do their duty purposefully, and are attentive to orders and instructions. The one is a state of mind just as is the other, and every state of mind grows out of the past. A myriad factors contribute to discipline – old habit, confidence in one's fellows, belief in the importance of one's duty. Roman discipline came to be based on fear of consequences; it was axiomatic in the Roman army that the soldier should fear his officers more than the enemy, and Frederick the Great used the same method with the Prussian Guard. An enthusiast will charge into danger, but, once stopped, he is likely to run away, and, running away, he is as hard to stop as when he is charging. Fear and enthusiasm are narrow and precarious bases for discipline. Perhaps the principal element in the Marines' discipline was pride – pride in themselves, pride in the duty entrusted them, pride in the cause in which they fought, and pride in the Navy in which they served.

The Torpedo Gunner's Mate indulged in none of these highly theoretical speculations. His glance round the Transmitting Station told him that the men were doing their duty, and gratified his curiosity; and a glance at Mr Kaile told him that all the apparatus was functioning correctly, thanks to the electricity which he was supplying to them. In reply to the Torpedo Gunner's Mate's lifted eyebrows, Mr Kaile gave a nod, and, having no more excuse to linger, the Torpedo Gunner's Mate withdrew to his action station.

'Nosey old bastard,' said Mr Kaile; he said it half to himself, but the other half into the telephone, and he had to add hastily to the Gunnery Lieutenant who heard it, 'Sorry, sir, I wasn't speaking to you.'

The telephone gurgled back at him with the information that *Artemis* was turning again to the attack.

'Yes, sir,' said Mr Kaile.

Mr Kaile's war experience went back twenty-eight years. At the battle of the Falkland Islands as a very young Ordinary Seaman he had played an undistinguished part, being merely one of the hands in HMS *Kent* who had been used as living ballast, sent aft with every man who could be spared from his station to stand on the quarterdeck so as to help lift the bows a trifle and add to the speed of the ship in her desperate pursuit of *Nürnberg*. Mr Kaile had stood there patiently while *Kent* plunged through the drizzling rain of that dramatic evening, and he had cheered with the others when *Nürnberg*, shot to pieces, had sunk into the freezing South Atlantic.

He had married a girl when at last *Kent* reached England again, Bessie – Bessie had been no oil-painting even then, as Mr Kaile politely described her looks to himself, but it was largely owing to Bessie that Mr Kaile now held his present exalted rank, with a 'Mr' before his name and a gold stripe on his sleeve. Oil-painting or not, Mr Kaile had loved Bessie from the first, and had never ceased to love her, with her gentleness and sympathy and her unbounded faith in her husband. Nothing was too good for Bessie. On Bessie's account Mr Kaile had become a man of towering ambition, with dreams that he hardly dared admit even to himself; even he had never ventured so far into the realms of the wildly improbable as to imagine his holding commissioned rank, but some of his dreams had been almost equally fantastic – he had dreamed of Bessie living in a house of their own, a house bought and paid for with the money he earned, and filled with furniture, *good* furniture, on which all the instalments were paid. It was too lofty a dream that Bessie should have a maid in the house, wearing cap and apron, but Mr Kaile certainly had aspired in those old days to Bessie's having a charwoman to do the rough work of the dream house – a respectable old body who would call Mrs Kaile 'Mum'. Mr Kaile as a young Leading Seaman had thrilled to the idea of someone doing that, but when he spoke of it to his wife she had only smiled tolerantly and stroked his hair as if he were a child telling about fairies.

And Leading Seaman Kaile had gone back to sea with the ambition rooted more deeply still, to earn his first medal by the way he handled a machine gun on the deck of the old *Vindictive* when she lay against Zeebrugge Mole with her upper works being torn to splinters by the German artillery. The ambition had stayed with him when the war ended, and sustained him through the years of the peace, while he slaved to supplement an elementary education and master the complexities (complexities which grew ever more complex) of the technical side of gunnery. Mr Kaile was not a brilliant man, but he was a man willing to go to endless effort, and under the stimulus of his ambition his mind grew more and more retentive in its memory for elaborate detail, and more and more orderly in its processes. He fell naturally into the discipline of HMS *Excellent*, and when the text-books that he read went beyond his comprehension he turned patiently back again to page one and started afresh analysing each sentence until he had cleared up the difficulty. He acquired the most complex assortment of rule of thumb knowledge, from the temperature at which cordite should be stored in a magazine to the breaking strain of chain cable. There was no gun in use in the British Navy which he could not repair or serve. He made orderly thinking an efficient substitute for the higher mathematics which he could never hope to learn, so that he could deal with muzzle velocities and trajectories in a workmanlike fashion. And he had risen from Leading Seaman to Petty Officer, and from Petty Officer to warrant rank, until at last he was what he had never hoped to be, a Commissioned Gunner, Mr Kaile; and Bessie lived in her own house – Mr Kaile deeded it over to her the day he paid the last instalment – full of her own furniture, and two days a week, before the war began in 1939, she had a charwoman in who called her 'Mum' to do the washing and the rough work. Mr Kaile did not know whether after the war there would be any servants again who would wear cap and apron, but so many unbelievable things had happened to him in his career that he had even thought this might be possible some day, and that he might have the last, ultimate pleasure of sitting in Bessie's own sitting-room hearing Bessie give instructions to her own servant.

Even without that prospect, merely to keep Bessie in her own house and surrounded by her own furniture, Mr Kaile would fight every Wop in the Eyety navy. He had realized so many of his ambitions, with Bessie undisputably leader of society in the circles in which she moved as wife of a Commissioned Gunner she could queen it, if she willed, over the wives of Chief Petty Officers and Sergeants of Marines. In point of fact, Bessie did not queen it very obviously, as Mr Kaile had noticed just as he noticed everything nice about Bessie. The pleasure for Mr Kaile lay in knowing that she could if she wanted to. Mr Kaile's present position, sitting at the head of the table in the Transmitting Station, was closely enough related in Mr Kaile's mind with the continuance of that pleasure.

Mr Kaile was fully aware that the Eyeties had good machinery of their own. He had read with the utmost care the confidential notes which had been circulated to gunnery officers in the Royal Navy regarding the discoveries made in captured Italian ships. Captured submarines had contributed a little – the submersible six-inch gun mounting was a most ingenious adaptation of an idea which the Navy had been (in Mr Kaile's mind) a little premature in discarding – and the destroyer captured in the Red Sea had told much more. Reconstructing in theory the Italian system of gunnery control in big ships from what could be seen in a destroyer was a sort of Sherlock Holmes job, like guessing a man's height from the length of his stride between footprints, and it was just the sort of thing Mr Kaile was good at. In his pocket at that moment there was a nice letter from the Lords Commissioners of the Admiralty thanking Mr Kaile for some suggestions he had made on the subject. One of these days the English would lay their hands on an intact Italian cruiser, or even a battleship – Mr Kaile hoped when that happened he would be there to see. It would be pretty good material, Mr Kaile was sure, but Mr Kaile was not so wrapped up in materials as to be unaware that the best of material is still dependent on men to be handled properly. He looked down the double row of serious faces along the Transmitting Station table and was satisfied. These kids were sometimes inclined to a frivolity which needed restraint. They were well enough behaved; when the big explosion had come, and the ship had jerked as if she had struck a rock, the lights had gone out instantly. But when they had come on again (Mr Kaile gave grudging credit to the Torpedo Gunner's Mate for the promptitude with which the circuits had been restored) they were still all sitting in their places, and each had reported quietly that the pointer each was observing was still functioning. They were quite steady, and Mr Kaile was human enough to realize that they might not be so in that atmosphere, for some freak of the ship's ventilation was dragging into the Transmitting Station a horrible stench – of burning paint, perhaps, but with other elements added; possibly burning meat. Mr Kaile could be single-minded and ignore that stench, and he could control his thoughts so as not to speculate about what might be happening elsewhere in the ship to cause that stench, but he knew that might not be the case with these lads. He was glad to see that it was.

'Enemy in sight. Green four-o,' said the telephones to Mr Kaile.

'All guns load,' said Mr Kaile to the turrets. That was an automatic reaction. The Transmitting Station was as quiet as a church, save for the curt sentences passing back and forth. Band Corporal Jones at his telephone was receiving, and repeating aloud, the enemy's course and deflection, as the Rate Officer announced it. The marvellous machines were making their calculations. Mr Kaile swept his eye over the table.

'Table tuned for deflection, sir,' he reported.

'Broadsides,' said the telephone back to him.

'Broadsides,' repeated Mr Kaile to the turrets.

A gong pealed sharply, and then *Artemis* heaved beneath their feet to her own broadside, and the rigid steel of her structure transported the din and the shock of the explosion into the Transmitting Station, astoundingly. And the new data began to pour into the Transmitting Station, and the pointers moved, tracked steadily by the Marine band, while every ten seconds came the crash of the broadside, and the stench from the burning wardroom flat seeped down into the Transmitting Station, polluting their nostrils.

19

From the Captain's Report

. . . so that the ship was ready to attack again . . .

The battle was approaching a climax. The wind had steadily rolled the smoke screen down upon the Italian battle line, and the British ships had advanced with it, nearer and nearer to the Italian ships. The Captain on the bridge of *Artemis* was considering the possibilities and potentialities of an attack by the destroyers with torpedoes. A destroyer is even more fragile than a light cruiser, and her attack must be launched only after careful preparation of it to be successful. At more than five thousand yards her torpedoes are running too slowly to have much chance of hitting a well-handled target, and the longer the range the more difficult it is to send the torpedo near the target. Fired at a line of ships, a salvo of torpedoes nominally stands a chance of hitting with one torpedo in three, because between each pair of ships there is an empty space twice as long as any ship, but slow torpedoes and alert handling makes this chance far slighter.

A forty-knot torpedo fired at a range of three miles at a ship advancing at twenty knots reaches its target in three minutes having only travelled two miles; but if the ship is retreating instead of advancing the torpedo must run for nine minutes, travelling six miles, before it overtakes its target. So a torpedo attack must always be delivered from ahead of the enemy's line, and it must be pressed home to the farthest limit in the teeth of the enemy's fire. That Italian battle line mounted over a hundred guns, which each fired a shell big enough to cripple a destroyer, over ranges at least three times as long as the maximum efficient torpedo range; if the destroyers were to launch a simple attack they would have a long and perilous gauntlet to run before they could fire their torpedoes with any hope of success. In fact, if even one of the six available destroyers got within torpedo range it would be surprising. And if, more surprisingly, that one destroyer had the opportunity to send off six torpedoes the chances would be against scoring two hits, and even two hits would probably not sink one of those big fellows over there. So the net result would be the loss of six destroyers in exchange for a temporary crippling of one or two major Italian units – a very bad bargain in the beggar-your-neighbour game of war.

The Captain had no need to recapitulate all this in his mind; his reasoning processes started at this point, up to which the facts were as much part of his mental equipment as a musician's knowledge of the number of flats in a scale. For the destroyers to stand any chance of success in the attack which the leader's flag signals were proposing to him the Italians must be distracted, their attention diverted and their aim divided. That meant launching another attack with the cruisers through the smoke screen so that they could attract the Italian fire to themselves, and then the destroyers could slip round the end of the screen ahead of the Italians and charge in. The Italian reply to this would be to keep their big guns firing at the cruisers and turn their secondary armament against the destroyers; but the Captain doubted whether in the stress of action the Italian fire control would be effective enough to master this added complication. And when the Italians attempted it they would be under the rapid fire of the British cruisers, shaken by hits and blinded by splashes. Some of their secondary armament, behind thin armour, might be put out of action – by some good fortune perhaps even the secondary gunnery control in some of the ships might be knocked out by lucky shells. That would make all the difference in the world. Another attack of the cruisers would increase the stake thrown on the board – exposing them again to the Italian fire at ever-lessening range – but it increased the chances of success to a far greater proportion. It made a good gamble of it.

The Captain pulled himself up sharply; his thoughts were running away with themselves. He was allowing himself to be carried away by his emotions. The realization was thrust upon him by the discovery that he was pleased with the prospect of plunging once more through the smoke screen, of being deafened again by the guns of *Artemis*, of seeing the shells he fired striking the Italian line. There was pleasure in the thought, and that meant danger. The Captain was a man of violent passions, although no mere acquaintance would ever have guessed it. People said that 'Methy' – Captain the Hon. Miles Ernest Troughton-Harrington-Yorke – had ice water in his veins instead of the blue blood one would expect of the son of the tenth Viscount Severne, but the people who said so did not know him, however close their acquaintance with him. The fact that he had a nickname should have warned them of the contrary, for even when their initials run together so conveniently, nicknames are not given to men who are as cold and hard and unemotional as they thought the Captain to be. As a boy and a youth Methy had indulged and indulged again in the rich dark pleasure of insane evil temper. He had revelled in the joy of having no bounds to his passion, of every restraint cast aside – the sort of joy whose intensity not even the drunkard or the drug-addict can know. One of Methy's brothers carried to his grave the scar across his scalp which resulted from a blow Methy dealt him – a blow not dealt to kill, for in his rage Methy never stopped to think of the possibility of killing, but a blow that might have killed. Methy's brother carried that scar to his grave, the unmarked grave amidst the shattered ruins of Boulogne where he fought to the last with the Guards.

Methy's wife knew about the frightful passions that could shake the man, for she had seen something of them. She could remember the young Lieutenant about to sail for the East Indian Station, frantic with jealousy that duty was taking him to the other side of the world while his rival stayed in England. He had been brutal, violent, demanding that she swear to be faithful to him, and she had been cold, aloof – concealing her fright – reminding him that they were not married or betrothed and that she had no intention of being either as long as he behaved like a madman.

That had been a very late manifestation of passion,

called forth by his love for a woman; long before that he had come to realize the insidious danger of a lack of self-control, and the insidious habit that could be formed by self-indulgence, more binding even than a drunkard's. He had mastered his passions, slowly and determinedly. Luckily he had matured early; luckily the discipline of the life of a naval cadet had been reinforced by the discipline of the life of a poor man's son – the tenth Viscount Severne had no money to speak of, and his three elder sons were in the army. When Gieves's agent came on board at Gibraltar and displayed shocked disapproval of jacket or cap, Methy had to smile and refuse to take the easy step of ordering new ones; when his rivals thought nothing of dinner at the Savoy or the Berkeley he had to suggest Soho. And he had come through without becoming either embittered or inhuman. Only a very few people knew that the Captain, good humoured, easy going in everything unconnected with the Service, witty and reliable and even tempered, had been compelled to learn to be each of these things; and most people who were in that secret thought the change was absolutely permanent. They looked upon Methy as an extinct volcano; but he himself knew, only too well, that he was only a dormant volcano, that mad rage could still master him – like some half-tamed animal it would still rise against him the moment he took his eye off it.

So the Captain regarded with suspicion his decision in favour of attacking the Italians again; warned by the surge of fighting madness in his brain he waited to cool off before reconsidering. He turned on his stool and looked about him at the homely and familiar surroundings, at the Torpedo Lieutenant and the Navigating Lieutenant and at Jerningham, at the compass and the voice pipes and the hasty after-thought of the Asdic cabinet. That had been hurriedly knocked together of three-ply; the Captain clairvoyantly foresaw a day when peace-time warships would have Asdic cabinets beautifully constructed of teak, elaborately polished and varnished. Three-ply was good enough for a light cruiser which might not be afloat by evening.

The fighting madness passed, his emotions under control again, the Captain reconsidered the idea of covering the destroyers' attack with the cruiser's fire. It was sound enough; the balance sheet of possible losses weighed against the chances of possible gains showed a profit. It was worth doing. Yet before deciding on a plan, it was as well to think about the enemy's possible plans; the Italians the other side of the smoke screen might be making some movement which could entirely nullify the destroyer attack, and they might also have up their sleeves some counter-move which could bring disaster on the cruiser squadron. The Captain thought seriously about it; if the Italian Admiral had any tactical sense he would have turned towards the smoke screen so that when the British ship emerged again they would find him not ten thousand yards, but only five thousand yards away; at that range the Italian salvoes could hardly miss. In a five-minute advance the Italians could reach the smoke screen, and in another minute they could be through it, with the convoy in sight and in range of their heavy guns. There might be a mêlée in the smoke screen at close quarters, where chance could play a decisive part, and where a light cruiser would be as valuable as a battleship. But chance was always inclined to favour the bigger squadrons and the bigger ships. The Italians could afford to lose heavily if in exchange they could destroy the British squadron first and the convoy, inevitably, later. Malta was worth a heavy cruiser or two or even a battleship. Far more than that; Malta was worth every ship the Italians had at sea, whether the island fortress were considered as the bastion of defence of the Eastern Mediterranean – as it was today – or as the advanced work from which an attack could be launched upon Italy – as it would be tomorrow.

It was only logical that the Italians should plunge forward into the attack – even if there were no other motive than the maintenance of the morale and the self-respect of the Italian crews, shaken by Matapan and Taranto and doomed to utter ruin if once more the Italian high command refused action with a greatly inferior force. That was all logical; the Captain reminded himself, smiling bleakly, that in war logic can be refuted by new arguments, and courage and dash on the part of the light cruisers could supply those. Time was passing, and the sun was sinking lower towards the horizon. The Italians had frittered time away. Even if now they made up their minds to attack there was a bare chance that a well-fought rearguard action might save the convoy – the British ships that survived the smoke screen action might lay another screen, and, when that was pierced, another yet, and so on, until sunset. A bare chance, but it was a chance.

The flagship astern, re-emerging from the smoke screen, was flashing a searchlight signal to *Artemis*, and the Captain heard the Chief Yeoman read off the letters one by one. By the time the message was one-third completed the Captain could guess what the end of it was going to be. The Admiral had reached the same decision regarding the destroyer attack as had the Captain, and this was the order putting into effect the plans discussed so long ago in contemplation of this very state of affairs.

'Acknowledge,' said the Captain to the Chief Yeoman of Signals, and then, to the Navigating Lieutenant, 'We'll attack again, Pilot. Starboard ten.'

20

From the Captain's Report

. . . and the attack was made . . .

'X' turret was not under the command of a commissioned officer. The Gunnery Lieutenant had found a kindred spirit in his chief gunner's mate; Allonby was one of those inspired fighting men – the Gunnery Lieutenant was another good example – that England produces in such numbers. At twenty-four, with his profound gunnery experience and his powers of leadership, Allonby had a career before him. Chief Petty Officer now, he was obviously destined to be commissioned Sub-Lieutenant shortly and Lieutenant immediately after, as soon as he should fill in the gaps in his technical education. The Captain had his eye on Allonby as a future Admiral. 'Aft through the hawse hole' the expression went, for describing the promotion of a man from the lower deck. Allonby would start with a handicap of six years in age, but prompt promotion would soon remedy that. No one could ever be quite sure how a man would react to promotion and added responsibility; Allonby might be a disappointment, but the Captain did not think it probable. On the contrary, he confidently expected that Allonby would clear all the hurdles before him and that one of these days Rear-

Admiral Allonby would hoist his flag in command of a squadron. But that was part of the problematical future. In the pressing, concrete present, Allonby was in command of 'X' turret. He was a hard man and a good-tempered man simultaneously, with no mercy for any lazy or careless individual who came under his orders; a martinet despite his ease of manner and his unconstrained good humour. The energetic men of 'X' turret's crew liked him and admired him; the lazy ones admired him equally and liked him nearly as much despite themselves. It had not been easy for Allonby; the man promoted from the lower deck to a post of great power and responsibility has to face a certain amount of inevitable friction with his subordinates. His good temper was only partly responsible for his success with his men; the most potent factor was his consistency. The man who smarted under Allonby's reprimands or who went under punishment as a result of his charges could see clearly enough that Allonby was not gratifying his own ego, or asserting himself in beggar-on-horseback fashion. There was nothing moody about Allonby. He worked steadily for the efficiency of 'X' turret, and he worked for it in the same way every day. He might rule 'X' turret with a rod of iron, but it was always a rod of iron, not a rod of iron one day and a rod of clay the next.

Even Ordinary Seaman Triggs could appreciate that fact, dimly and without understanding. Triggs was the ship's bad character, careless, lazy, drunken, stupid, dirty – possessed, in other words, of all the qualities likely to get him into trouble. Most likely Triggs was of an intelligence well below standard, having slipped through the

Navy's tests by misfortune or oversight. In civil life he would have sunk to the lowest levels of society, or rather have stayed there, among the shiftless drunken dregs which gave him birth. As it was, the Navy could feed him and clothe him, build up his physique and keep him at work which was not too exacting, but even the Navy could not give him the intelligence to profit by all this. His limited brain was almost incapable of grasping an order – the sharpest punishment could not impress upon him the necessity for listening to what he was told to do and then doing it. 'In at one ear and out at the other' as his exasperated shipmates said, and some would add that this was because there was nothing between his ears to act as an impediment. Five minutes after the six-inch guns' crews had been told to fall in for exercise the ship's loudspeaker would always say 'Ordinary Seaman Triggs, close up,' and it might even be two or three times that Ordinary Seaman Triggs was ordered to close up before he came tumbling aft to 'X' turret, his usual inane grin on his face, while Chief Petty Officer Allonby fumed and seethed. Time and place meant nothing to him. As a confirmed leave-breaker he rarely could be trusted ashore; when, after months on board perforce, he had at last purged himself of the sin of leave-breaking and was allowed on shore, it was only to be brought back by the naval police, hideously drunk and long overdue, to begin the weary cycle over again. There was always something of Triggs's in the ship's scranbag – lost property office – it was always Triggs who had to be told to get his hair cut or his nails cleaned. Captain and Commander had learned to sigh when they saw his name among the ship's defaulters and had him brought up before them, the silly smile on his face and his fingers twining aimlessly as he held his cap. The Captain had set in motion the official mechanism which would bring about Triggs's discharge from the Navy as unlikely to become an efficient seaman, but in time of war, with every man needed, and a personnel of a million men to be administered, the mechanism moved slowly, and Triggs was still on board *Artemis* when the battle was fought which decided the fate of the Mediterranean.

Allonby had stationed Triggs down in the magazine of 'X' turret, along with the officers' steward and the other untrained men, where he could do no harm. It was odd to think of Triggs put among tons of high explosive deliberately, but it was perfectly correct that he was harmless there, for cordite is a stubborn material. It will burn readily enough, but nothing save high pressure or another explosive will induce it to explode. As long as there was no chance of their catching fire the big cylinders of high explosive which Triggs handled were as harmless as so many pounds of butter. In the magazine with Triggs was Supply Assistant Burney, with more brains and reliability, and what Triggs and Burney had to do when the guns were in action was to take the tin boxes one by one from the racks in the magazine, extract the cordite charges from the boxes, and pass the charges through the flash-tight shutter in the bulkhead into the handling-room. Every ten seconds the two guns fifty feet above their heads each fired a round; every ten seconds two cordite charges in the magazine had to be stripped of their tin cases and passed through the shutter. That was all that had to be done; possibly in the whole ship when she was in action there was no duty calling for less practice or intelligence. Supply Assistant Burney may have felt himself wasted in the after magazine, but his routine duties in the ship made it hard to train him for a more exacting task, and his friends told him cheerfully that he could devote any attention he had to spare to seeing that Triggs did not strike matches down there. How Burney actually spent his time during the long and dreary waits while the guns were not firing was in squatting on the steel deck, with a couple of tons of high explosive round him and the sea just outside, reading *Economics in Theory and Practice*, for Burney's hobby was economics and he had vague ideas about some sort of career when he should leave the Navy. And Triggs would whistle tunelessly, and fidget about the steel cell that enclosed them, and, possibly, think vaguely whatever thoughts may come by chance into such a mind as Triggs possessed. He would finger the telephone, and peer at the thermometer, and drum with his fingers on the bulkhead. It was always a relief to Burney when the gong jangled and the guns bellowed atrociously overhead and he and Triggs had to resume their task of passing cordite through the shutters.

Down here in the magazine the forced ventilation was always hard at work, for cordite is peculiarly susceptible to changes in temperature, and if the after magazine was ever warmer or colder than the forward magazine the six guns would not shoot identically, the broadsides would 'spread', and all the skill of the spotters, all the uncanny intelligence of the machines, all the training of the guns' crews, would be wasted. So the ventilators hummed their monotonous note as air from the outside was forced down, and with it came the greasy smoke of the smoke screen, and the sickening stench from the burnt-out wardroom flat. For the fifth time now the oil smoke was being drawn into the magazine, as *Artemis* made her third attack, but Burney and Triggs had not troubled to count, and could not have guessed at the number of times; they were probably vaguer about the course of the battle than anyone else in the ship. Petty Officer Hannay, in the handing-room, had not much chance of telling them, during the brief seconds the flash-tight shutter was open, the news he heard over the loudspeaker. Burney had learned to be fatalistic about his ignorance, and Triggs did not care.

21

From the Captain's Report

. . . in support of the attack made by the destroyers . . .

The Captain made himself ready to meet any emergency as *Artemis* shot out of the smoke screen. Anything might be awaiting him on the other side. He might find himself right under the guns of the Italian battleships and heavy cruisers if they had moved forward to anticipate the attack. The Italian destroyers might be lurking in ambush beyond the smoke screen, ready to send in a salvo of torpedoes. It was hard to believe that the Italian battle line would remain on the defensive under the repeated goading of these attacks.

The smoke wreaths thinned, the blue sky overhead became visible, and there ahead was the Italian line, nine thousand yards away, still fumbling to find an unopposed path round the smoke screen that lay between them and their prey. The Captain kept his glasses on them as he gave his orders. It was the same line of battle – the two elephantine battleships in the van, massive and menacing, their silhouetted upper works showing no sign of damage at that distance, and the heavy cruisers in their wake, smoke coiling greasily from their funnels. The second cruiser in the line had other smoke leaking from her upper works – clear proof that a shell had got home somewhere in her.

Artemis came round on a parallel course, and her guns crashed out, the hot blast from them eddying over the bridge, the unbelievable noise of them beating against the eardrum of officers and men, and the faint smoke from the muzzles whirling by alongside. Through his glasses the Captain saw the long stout silhouettes of the leading battleship's big guns against the horizon. Slowly they shortened as the turrets trained round. They disappeared behind a screen of splashes as *Artemis*'s broadside struck – through the splashes the Captain saw the gleam of a hit – and then when the splashes were gone the guns were still no longer visible, and the Captain knew that they were pointed straight at him. *Artemis* had fired two more broadsides, and at this range the shells reached the target a second before the next was fired. Splashes and flashes, smoke and spray made the battleship's outline uncertain, as the Captain held her in the field of his glasses, countering the roll and vibration of his own ship. But then the Captain saw, through all the vagueness, the sudden intense flames of the battleship's salvo. She had fired, and in that second the Captain was aware of four momentary black dots against the blue above her silhouette, come and gone so quickly that he could hardly be quite sure of what he had seen. It might be a subjective illusion, like the black spots that dance before the eyes in a bilious attack. This was no bilious attack; the Captain knew that what he had seen were the four big shells of the Italian's salvo on their way towards him, travelling faster than the speed of sound and charged with destruction and death. The Captain faced their coming unabashed and impersonal.

A hundred yards from *Artemis*'s starboard side rose the massive yellow columns of water; surprisingly, one big shell richocheted from the surface, bouncing up without exploding, turning end-over-end and travelling slowly enough for the eye to follow it as it passed fifty feet above *Artemis*'s stern. Everything was happening at once; a broadside from *Artemis* reached its target while the flash of the Italian salvo still lingered on the Captain's retina, and another was fired at the very moment that shell was passing overhead.

'Turn two points to starboard, Pilot,' said the Captain to the Navigating Lieutenant.

In response *Artemis* sheered towards the enemy's line, shortening the range. The Italian salvo had fallen short; they would lengthen the range for the next. The Captain saw the gleam of it, saw the black spots dance again before his eyes, and then he heard the rumble of the shells overhead, high-pitched for a moment and then dropping two tones in the musical scale as they passed to fling up their vast fountains a hundred and fifty yards to port; *Artemis* had ducked under the arc of their trajectory like a boxer under a punch.

'Four points to port, Pilot,' said the Captain.

The Italians would shorten their range this time, and *Artemis* must withdraw from the blow like a boxer stepping back. All this time her guns were bellowing in reply; the erratic course she was steering would make the Gunnery Lieutenant's task harder, because the range would be opening and closing for her just as much as for the Italians; but the Gunnery Lieutenant, and the machines in the Transmitting Station would be kept informed of the alterations of course, and would not have to guess at them – over in the Italian ships the Captain could imagine the inclinometer operators at work, peering at their smoke-wreathed, splash-surrounded target and trying to guess whether the vague image they saw was growing fatter or thinner. If *Artemis* zigzagged while the Italians maintained a steady course it would be to *Artemis*'s advantage, therefore, and she would have more chance of hitting than the Italians had; while if the Italians should decide to zigzag, too, it would merely make it harder for everyone so as to give the British superiority in training and discipline more opportunity still.

The Captain was handling his ship, watching the Italian gunnery and observing the effect of his own. He turned and looked aft; the other cruisers had broken through the smoke screen and were blazing away at the Italian line, a chain of Davids attacking Goliaths. He turned his attention forward again; that was where the destroyers would launch their attack as soon as the Italians were fully distracted by the light cruisers. It was a matter for the nicest judgement on the part of the destroyer leader, for the cruisers could not be subjected for too long to the fire of the Italian battle line. In the very nature of things, by pure laws of chance, one or other of those innumerable salvoes must strike home at last; he ordered a new change of course, and a sudden flash of thought set him smiling grimly again as it crossed his mind momentarily that perhaps, if the Italian spotters were rattled and the Italian gunnery officers unskilful, the 'short' might be corrected as if it were an 'over' and he might be steering right into the salvo instead of away from it. There was no predicting what unnerved men might do. But still it certainly could not be worse than pure chance, and the sea was wide and the spread even of an Italian salvo was small; the Captain's sane and sanguine temperament reasserted itself. Despite that tremendous din, with *Artemis* rolling in a beam sea, and with a dozen factors demanding his attention and his calculation, and in face of appalling odds it was necessary that he should remain both clear-headed and cheerful.

Jerningham behind the Captain felt physically exhausted. The noise and the nervous strain were wearing him down. This was the third time *Artemis* had emerged from the shelter of the smoke screen to run the gauntlet of the Italian salvoes. How many more times would they have to do this – how many more times would they be able to? He was tired, for many emotions had shaken him that day, from terror under the morning's bombing attack to exasperation at reading Dora Darby's letter, and thence to exultation after the first successful attack. Exultation was gone now, and he only knew lassitude and weariness. He felt he would give anything in the world if only this frightful din would stop and the terrible danger would cease. The hand which held the rail beside him was cramped with gripping tight, and his throat was so dry that although he tried to swallow he could not do so. His eyes were dry too, or so they felt – his lids wanted to droop down over them and seemed to be unable to do so because of the friction with the dry surface. He was caught between the upper millstone of the Captain's inflexible will and the nether millstone of the Italian invulnerability.

It was a six-inch shell that hit the cruiser eventually,

fired perhaps, from the Italian flagship's secondary armament, or maybe a chance shot from one of the cruisers. The chances of dynamics dictated that it did not deal the *Artemis* nearly as severe a shock as the previous hit had done, although it caused far more damage. It struck the ship's side a yard above the water line abreast of 'X' turret, and it penetrated the main deck as it burst, flinging red-hot fragments of steel all round it. Beneath the main deck there was No. 7 fuel tank containing fifty tons of oil fuel, and the shell ripped it open as it set everything ablaze. Oil welled up into the blaze and blazed itself, and the heat generated by the fire set more and more of the expanding oil welling up to feed the fire. The roll of the ship sent the burning oil running over the decks, turning the after-part of the ship into one mass of flames.

It was not merely the oil which burnt; it was not merely No. 7 fuel tank which was ripped open by the flying red-hot steel. Inboard of where the shell struck was 'X' turret, and from 'X' turret downwards to the bottom of the ship extended the ammunition supply arrangements for the turret – the lobby below the gunhouse and the magazine below the lobby. Fragments of the shell came flying through that thin steel of the bulkhead of 'X' turret lobby, and with the fragments came the flame of the explosion. The rating at the shell ring, the rating at the ammunition hoist, fell dead at their posts, killed by the jagged steel, and the petty officer in charge of the lobby, and the other ratings survived them only by a second. They died by fire, but it was a quick death. One moment they were alive and hard at work; the next, and the cordite charge in the hoist had caught alight and was spouting flames which filled full the whole interior of the lobby. One quick breath, and the men who took that breath fell dead. It was their dead bodies upon which the flame then played, so hot that the bodies were burned away in smoke and gas during the few seconds that the ammunition blaze lasted. Lobby and crew were wiped out; of the crew nothing remained – nothing – and of the lobby only the red-hot steel box, its sides warped and buckled with the heat.

On the bridge the shock of the blow passed nearly unfelt; the crash of the explosion nearly unheard. Jerningham saw the Chief Yeoman of Signals, on the wing of the bridge, looking anxiously aft. Where Jerningham stood the funnels and superstructure blocked the view astern, and he walked to the side and leaned over, craning his neck to look aft. Dense black smoke was pouring out of the side of the ship and was being rolled by the wind towards the enemy, and as Jerningham looked he saw massive flames sprouting at the root of the smoke, paling as a trick of the wind blew the smoke away, reddening as the smoke screened the sunshine from them. It was a frightening sight.

'Turn two points to starboard, pilot,' said the Captain to the Navigating Lieutenant; he was still handling his ship to avoid the shells raining round her, unconscious of what had happened. Jerningham saluted to catch his attention, and the Captain turned to him.

'Ship's on fire aft, sir,' said Jerningham. His voice quavered, and was drowned as he spoke by the roar of the guns. He repeated himself, more loudly this time, and the need to speak more loudly kept his voice steady.

It was two full seconds before the Captain spoke, and then it was only one word, which meant nothing.

'Yes?' said the Captain.

'Pretty badly, apparently, sir,' said Jerningham. Exasperation at the Captain's dullness put an edge to his voice.

'Very good, Jerningham, thank you,' said the Captain.

The guns bellowed again, their hot blast whirling round the bridge.

'The reports will come in soon,' said the Captain. 'Pilot, turn four points to port.'

On the instant he was immersed again in the business of handling the ship. The destroyers were at this very moment dashing out of their ambush round the end of the smoke screen, and this was the time for them to be given all possible support. As long as the guns would fire, as long as the ship would answer her helm, she must be kept in the fighting line – for that matter she must be kept in the fighting line anyway, if for no other reason than to attract to herself as much of the Italian fire as possible. The fact that she was a mass of flames aft did not affect the argument. Whether she was doomed to blow up, or whether eventually she was going to sink, had no bearing on the present. She would or she would not. Meanwhile, there went the destroyers.

The Captain fixed his glasses on them. The attack had been well judged, and the destroyers were racing down to meet the Italians on a course converging at an acute angle. They were going at their highest speed – even at this distance the Captain could see their huge bow-waves, brilliant white against the grey; and their sterns had settled down so deep in the troughs they ploughed in the surface as to be almost concealed. The White Ensigns streamed behind them, and the thin smoke from their funnels lay above the surface of the sea in rigid parallel bars.

The Captain swung his glasses back to the Italian fleet, and from there to the other cruisers steaming briskly along with their guns blazing; for the first time he saw the dense smoke which was pouring out of *Artemis*'s quarter. He saw it, but his mind did not register the sight – the decision to take no action about the ship being on fire had already been made. He changed the ship's course again to dodge the salvoes and looked once more at the destroyers. His glasses had hardly begun to bear on them when he saw the sea all about them leap up into fountains – the Italians had at last opened fire on them. For a full minute of the necessary five that they must survive they had been unopposed. The destroyers began to zigzag; the Captain could see their profiles foreshortening first in one sense and then in the other as they turned from side to side like snipe under gunfire. Evasive action of that sort was a stern test of the gunners firing on them. Not merely was the range decreasing but the bearing was constantly altering – traversing a big gun back and forth to keep the sights on a little ship as handy as a destroyer, zigzagging under the unpredictable whim of her captain, was a chancy business at best.

It was important to note whether the Italian fire was accurate or not. The whole surface of the sea between the destroyers and the Italians was pock-marked with splashes, and far beyond the destroyers too. There were wild shots which threw up the sea hardly a mile from the Italians' bows, and there were wild shots falling three miles astern of the destroyers; over the whole of that length and making a zone a mile and a half wide, a hundred guns were scattering five hundred shells every minute, but the splashes were clustered more thickly about the destroyers than anywhere else – that much at least could be said for the Italian gunnery.

There were flashes darting from the destroyers, too. They were banging away with their 4.7-inch popguns – peashooters would not be much less effective against the massive steel sides of the Italian battleships, but there was always the chance of a lucky hit. The leading destroyer vanished utterly in a huge pyramid of splashes, and the Captain gulped, but two seconds later she emerged unharmed, her guns still firing, jinking from side to side so sharply that her freeboard disappeared as she lay over.

Jerningham was at the Captain's side again, with a report received by telephone.

'"X" turret reports they have flooded the magazine, sir,' said Jerningham to the Captain's profile.

'Thank you,' said the Captain without looking round.

If the after-magazine was flooded it would mean that the two guns in 'X' turret would be silent, that was all. There were still the four guns of 'A' and 'B' turrets in action, and four guns fired a large enough salvo for efficiency. *Artemis* would not blow up yet awhile, either; but as the Captain would not have varied his course of action even if he had been utterly certain that she was going to blow up in the next minute that did not matter.

The leading destroyer disappeared again in the

splashes, and reappeared again miraculously unhurt. The second destroyer in the line swung round suddenly at right angles, her bows pointed almost straight for *Artemis*. A cloud of white steam enveloped her, and then a moment or two later her black bows crept out of it and she began to crawl slowly away, steam and smoke still pouring from her as she headed for the shelter of the smoke screen. It was the first casualty; some shell had hit her in the boiler-room presumably. The other five were still tearing towards their objective; the Captain swung his glasses back at the Italian line in time to see a bright flash on the side of the Italian flagship – indisputably a hit and not gunfire, for it was a single flash – but he did not know enough about the broadsides *Artemis* had been firing to be able to credit it either to his own ship or to the destroyers. 'A' and 'B' turrets were still firing away, but, amazingly, the ears were so wearied by the tremendous sound that they took no special note of it unless attention was specially directed upon the guns.

By now the destroyers must be nearly close enough to discharge their torpedoes. The Captain tried to estimate the distance between them and their objective. Six thousand yards, maybe. Five thousand, perhaps – it was difficult to tell at that angle. The officers in command had displayed all the necessary courage and devotion. And the Italian destroyers were creeping out ahead of the Italian battle line to meet them now – they had been left behind when the Italian fleet turned about to try and work round the smoke screen, and had been compelled to sheer away widely to get on the disengaged side, and had then had to waste all those precious minutes working their way up to the head of the line where they should have been stationed all along. At the first hint of a British destroyer attack they should have been ready to move forward to fend it off, engaging with their own class beyond torpedo range of the battle line. The Captain fancied that there was a bad quarter-hour awaiting the senior Italian destroyer officer if ever he made port; he would probably be unjustly treated, but a naval officer who expected justice was expecting too much.

The leading British destroyer was wheeling round now, and the others were following her example, turning like swallows. Presumably at that moment the torpedoes were being launched, hurled from the triple tubes at the Italian line. Thirty torpedoes, the Captain hoped, were now dashing through the water, twenty feet below the surface against the Italians – sixty thousand pounds' worth of machinery thrown into the sea on the chance that five pounds' worth of TNT might strike home; that was as typical of war as anything he knew; the dive bombers he had beaten off that morning were a hundred times more expensive still.

He kept his glasses on the Italian line so as to make sure of the effect of the torpedo attack, even while, in the midst of the deafening din, he continued to handle his ship so as to evade the enemy's salvoes. He was wet through from the splash of a shell close overside, and his skin kept reporting to his inattentive mind the fact that it was clammy and cold, just as in the same way he had been listening to reports on the progress of the struggle to extinguish the fire aft. This was the crisis of the battle, the moment which would decide the fate of Malta and of the world. Whatever happened to that fire aft, he must keep his ship in action a little longer, keep his four remaining six-inch guns in action, not merely to cover the retirement of the destroyers but to out-face and out-brave that line of Italian capital ships.

22

From the Captain's Report

. . . the ship sustained another hit . . .

When that six-inch shell struck *Artemis*'s side they were hardly aware of it forward on the bridge, but aft in 'X' turret there could be no misunderstanding of what had happened – they heard the crash and felt the jar of the explosion, smelt the suffocating stench of high explosive and burning fuel, and saw the red flames that raged round them. Beneath their feet in the gunhouse they felt the whole structure stir uneasily, like the first tremor of an earthquake, but the guns' crews could not allow that to break the smooth rhythm of loading and firing – sliding shells and charges from the hoist to the breeches, inserting the tubes and masking the vents, closing the breeches and then swinging them open again. Yet something else broke that rhythm.

'Hoist's stopped working, Chief,' reported Number Two at the right-hand gun.

'Use the ready-use charges,' said Allonby.

Three rounds for each gun were kept in 'X' turret in contemplation of such an emergency – enough for half a minutes' firing. There is no point in keeping ammunition below the surface of the sea in the magazine and yet maintaining large quantitites of high explosive above decks behind a trivial inch of steel. And when dealing with high explosive – with cylinders of cordite that can spout flames a hundred feet long a second after ignition – thirty seconds is a long time.

Allonby bent to the steel voice pipe beside him which led down to the lobby beneath his feet. A blast of hot air greeted him, and he hastily restoppered the pipe, for actual flame might come through there. The turret walls were hot to the touch – almost too hot to touch; the gunhouse must be seated at that moment in a sea of flame. It was just as well they were firing off those ready-use rounds and getting rid of them the best possible way. The turret was filling with smoke so that they could hardly see or breathe. They could be suffocated or baked alive in this steel box; the party in the lobby below must have been killed instantly. The instinct of self-preservation would have driven Allonby and the guns' crews out of 'X' turret the moment those red flames showed through the slits. It would be hard to believe that flight was actually the last thought that occurred to them, except that our minds are dulled by tales of heroism and discipline. We hear so many stories of men doing their duty that our minds are biased in that direction. The miracle of men staying in the face of the most frightful death imaginable ceases to be a miracle unless attention is directly called to it. Undisciplined men, untrained men, would have seen those flames and felt that heat; they might have halted for one paralysed second, but the moment realization broke in upon them they would have fled in the wildest panic that nothing would have stopped – possibly not even the threat of a worse fate (if one could be imagined) than being baked to death in a steel box. In 'X' turret under Allonby's leadership the thought of flight occurred to no one; they went on loading and reloading. Allonby had to take the decision that would make his turret utterly useless, even if the lobby and the hoist could be repaired; he had to relegate himself from being the proud captain of 'X' turret into the position of being a mere passenger at the same time as he put one-third of the main armament of *Artemis* out of action for good. He had to bear all the responsibility himself; with that fire blazing there was not even time to ask permission from the Gunnery Lieutenant.

Allonby seized the voice pipe to the magazine, and to his intense relief it was answered; Allonby knew Burney's voice as he knew the voice of every man under his command.

'Flood the magazine,' said Allonby.

'Flood the magazine?'

There was a question mark at the end of the sentence – it was not the usual Navy repetition of an order. The crash of the firing of the next round made Allonby pause for a second before he repeated himself, slowly and distinctly, making quite sure that he was understood. The last round was fired from the guns as he plugged the voice pipe.

'Clear the turret,' said Allonby to his men, and they began to scramble out, leaping, through the flames to safety as if it were some ceremonial worship of Moloch.

Allonby applied himself to the telephone. The Gunnery Lieutenant and the Transmitting Station must know at once that 'X' turret had ceased to fire; otherwise both the control and the spotting of the other guns would suffer. When he had finished that it was too late to escape from the turret, which was ringed with fire now and whose steel plates were red hot.

And down below the main deck, below the water line, Ordinary Seaman Triggs and Supply Assistant Burney came out from the magazine into the handling-room and from there into the alleyway along with the handling-room crew. The elaborate mechanisms which had been specially designed for this emergency had played their part in saving the ship from instant destruction. All the way along the chain of ammunition supply, from magazine and shell-room to handling-room, from handling-room to lobby, from lobby to turret, there were flash-proof doors and shutters. At Jutland twenty-six years ago, similar hits had resulted in the destruction of three big battle cruisers; the roaring flames of one ignited charge had flashed from one end to the other, from turret to magazine, setting off the tons of high explosive in a blast which had blown the huge ships to fragments. In *Artemis* only the lobby had been wiped out, and only two charges had added their hundred-foot flames to those of the burning fuel. The flash-proof doors had allowed time, had stretched the period during which safety action could be taken from one-tenth of one second to fifteen seconds – time for Allonby to give his orders; possibly time for Burney or Triggs to carry them out. The alleyway in which the group found themselves was a place of unimaginable horror. It was filled with dense smoke, but no smoke could be thick enough to hide the scene entirely. Through holes in the torn deck above long tongues of red flame were darting intermittently down from the blazing lobby. At the end of the alleyway the bursting shell had blown bulkheads and doors into a porcupine-tangle of steel blades which protruded from a burning sea of oil; and with every movement of the ship the surface lapped over them and the flames ran farther down the alleyway. The heat was terrific, and although the flames were distinct enough the smoke was so thick that only objects directly illuminated by them were visible – the men groped about blinded, their lungs bursting and their eyes streaming.

'Flood the magazine!' shouted Burney in the fog. He ran round to where the twin wheels were which operated the inlet valves, with Triggs behind him; they ran through thin fire. Burney laid his hands on the wheels.

He had been drilled as far as this. Among the innumerable gunnery drills, RI exercises and sub-calibre work, sometimes the order had come through 'Clear "X" turret. Flood the magazine,' and Burney had run to the valves, even as he had now, and laid his hands on the wheels, as he did now, with Triggs beside him. Mechanical arrangements for flooding magazines might as well not exist if a man were not detailed to operate them, and practised in what he had to do; and not one man, but two, for men may die in the Navy.

But in this case action was different from practice, for the wheels were too hot to touch. Involuntarily Burney snatched his hands back from them with a cry of pain. They were seared and burnt. A sluggish river of burning oil trickled towards them and stopped five feet from them. Burney put his hands to the wheels again, but when he put his weight on his hands to force the wheels round it was more than his will would endure. He cried out with pain, agonized. Blind reflexes made him put his charred hands under his armpits as he stamped with agony and the burning oil edged nearer to him.

Cordite is a touchy substance, impatient of bonds. Free from confinement it will submit to rough treatment; it can be dropped, or thrown or tossed about without resenting the indignity. It will even burn, two out of three times, without exploding – a block consuming itself in a second, which is its approximate rate of combustion, instead of in a hundredth of a second, which is its rate of explosion. But if it is compressed or confined it will resent it vigorously. A pinch of fulminate then will make it explode, the wave of explosion jumping from molecule to molecule through the whole mass with the speed of light. And cordite is touchy about the temperature at which it is kept, too – let that rise a few degrees, and it begins to decompose. Nitrous fumes begin to rise from it; strange, complex, unstable nitrous acids begin to form within it. It begins to heat itself up spontaneously, accelerating the process in a vicious circle. So that if its temperature is allowed to rise while at the same time it is kept confined a pressure is developed which increases by leaps and bounds, and the decomposing cordite, compressed beyond all bounds, will explode without waiting for a primer to set it off.

Within 'X' turret magazine temperature and pressure were rising rapidly as the magazine's bulkheads passed on their heat to the cordite within. Thick yellow fumes (although there was no human eye within to see them) were flooding into the magazine as the unstable molecules stirred restlessly. A blast was approaching which would tear the ship in two, which might wipe out every human life within her. Pressure was piling up. Ordinary Seaman Triggs heard Burney's cries; the flames from the burning oil dimly illuminated Burney's shadowy figure bowed over his charred hands. Drill and discipline had left mark even on Trigg's vague mental make-up. He knew orders were meant to be obeyed, although it was so easy to forget them and so easy to be distracted from their execution. When he went on shore he never meant to overstay his leave; it was only that he forgot; only that drink confused and muddled him. When the order came over the loudspeaker '"X" turret crew close up,' he would always obey it promptly except that he was so often thinking about something else. Here amid the smoke and flame of the alleyway, Triggs, oddly enough, was thinking about nothing except the business in hand. He saw Burney try to turn the wheels and fail, and without hesitation he took up the task. The pain in his hands was frightful, but Triggs was able to ignore it. He flung his weight on the wheels and they moved; again and again they moved, turning steadily.

Temperature in the magazine was high; there was a red danger mark on the thermometer hung within and the mercury was far, far above it. Pressure was high, too. Triggs turned the wheels, the steel rods rotated, the worm-gear turned, and the inlet valves in the magazine slowly opened to admit the sea. Momentarily there was a strange reluctance on the part of the sea to enter; the pressure within was so high that the twelve feet below water line of the valves did not give enough counter-pressure to force the water in. Then *Artemis* rolled, rolling the valves three feet further below the surface, and that added pressure just sufficed. Two jets of water sprang up into the magazine, greedily absorbing the yellow nitrous fumes and cooling the heated gas so that the pressure within the magazine dropped abruptly; even when *Artemis* went back to an even keel the sea still welled up into the magazine, and when she heeled over the next time the jets spouted far higher, cooling and absorbing so that now the sea rushed in like a flood, filling the whole magazine.

Triggs knew now that his hands hurt him; the charred bones were visible where the flesh of his palms had been burned away. He was sobbing with pain, the sobs rising to a higher and higher pitch as the pain grew more intense and the realization of it more and more acute; wounds in the hand seem to be especially unnerving and painful, presumably because of the ample nerve supply to their surfaces. Burney mastered his own agony for a space, sufficient to lead Triggs forward to the sickbay where Sick Berth Petty Officer Webster was doing his best to attend to the wounded who were being brought in here now that the wardroom and the Surgeon Lieutenant-Commander had been wiped out. Webster could at least bandage those frightful hands, and at least could give morphia to check those high-pitched sobs of Triggs's.

And meanwhile the Commander and his men, with 'X' turret's crew to help, and Sub-Lieutenant Richards with such of his men as the shell had left alive, battled with hoses and chemical extinguishers against the sea of flames that had engulfed the after half of the ship, reducing it bit by bit from a sea to a lake, from a lake to isolated pools, until at last the tons of sea water which the pumps brought on board had extinguished every spark.

23

From the Captain's Report

... with moderate damage ...

When the crew of *Artemis* was at action stations one of the loneliest men in the ship was Henry Hobbs, Stoker First Class. His station was in the shaft tunnel, aft, a watertight door behind him and a watertight door in front of him, cutting him off from the rest of the world, and his duty was to watch over the eight shaft-bearings and to see that they did not run hot. The shaft tunnel was an inch less than five feet in height, so that Hobbs walked about in it bent double; and it was lighted eerily by a few sparse electric bulbs, and when *Artemis* was under full power, as she had been during this battle, the tunnel was full of the incessant high-pitched note of the shaft, which in that confined space made a continuous noise of a tone such as to make the unaccustomed listener feel he could not bear to listen to it any longer. Stoker Hobbs was used to it; in fact, it might as well be said he liked the noise and that it was no hardship for him to be stationed in the shaft tunnel; it must be further admitted that when action stations were being allotted Hobbs had looked so earnestly at Stoker Petty Officer Harmsworth so as to attract his attention and gain his influence in his favour in the matter. Harmsworth had cheerfully put forward Hobbs's name for duty in the tunnel because Hobbs was essentially reliable. It was unlikely that more than once in a watch an officer would come into the tunnel to inspect, so the stoker on duty there must be someone who could be trusted to do his duty without supervision.

The duty was not a very exacting one, because the main duty that Hobbs had to perform was to watch his eight bearings. He could tell by touch when one was running hot instead of warm, and he had exactly to anticipate this by opening the oil valve regulating the flow of lubricating oil to the bearing. The only other thing he had to do was to watch the bilge below the shaft – the ultimate lowest portion of the ship – and report if it began to deepen. The rest of the time Hobbs could spend in communion with God.

In Hobbs's opinion the shaft tunnel was the ideal place in which to address himself to God, and this opinion was the result of a large variety of factors. It was odd that the least potent of these factors was that he could be alone in the tunnel – solitude is something hard to find in a light cruiser crammed with a full wartime crew. The art of staying sane in a crowd, and of retaining one's individuality when living night and day shoulder to shoulder with one's fellows, has been perfected through generations of seamen since Drake in the give-and-take life of the lower deck, and a man has freedom enough to speak to God if he wishes to. The man who says his prayers is just another individual, as is the man who indulges in the almost forgotten habit of chewing tobacco, or the man who amazingly sleeps face downward in his hammock.

So solitude was to Hobbs's mind only the least attractive aspect of duty in the shaft tunnel – it was of some importance, but not of much. That continuous high-pitched hum was more important. Hobbs found that it led his mind towards the higher things of life. The finest organ playing in the world, the most impassioned sermons were less effective in this way than the note of the shaft as far as Hobbs was concerned. The vibration played its part, too; nowhere in the length and breadth and depth of HMS *Artemis* was the vibration as noticeable as in the shaft tunnel. That vibration, intense and rapid, always set Stoker Hobbs thinking about the wrath of God – the connexion could hardly be apparent to anyone else, but to Hobbs it was clear enough. It was important, for in Hobbs's mind God was a Being who was filled with implacable wrath – implacable towards Hobbs alone, as far as Hobbs knew or cared. It was none of Hobbs's concern how God felt towards all the other men who swarmed through the ship. The naked steel that surrounded Hobbs in the tunnel, and the dreary lighting – harsh patches of light and darkness – reminded Hobbs of God, too, and so did the cramped confinement, and the blind leaps and surges of the tunnel when the ship was in a sea-way. And when the guns were firing the sound of them, by some trick of acoustics, was carried through the steel framework of the ship to a focus in the tunnel, so that it resounded like a steel drainpipe pounded with sledgehammers.

From this picture of the shaft tunnel can be drawn a picture, then, of the aspect of God which Stoker Hobbs thought was turned towards him, seeing that it was here, amid the din and vibration, among these repulsive surroundings, that he thought he was nearest to Him. Hobbs would have been the first to agree, on the other hand, that this was definitely only one aspect of God; just as only one face of the moon is visible to us on earth, however the earth rotates and the moon revolves, so God steadily kept only one side of Him towards Hobbs; there was another, beneficent side which other and more fortunate people could see – just as from another planet the back of the moon is visible – but they were not such frightful sinners, such utterly lost souls as was Henry Hobbs.

Close questioning of him, by someone whom Hobbs could not suspect of flippancy or irreligion, would have elicited from him the fact – not the admission – that all these dreadful sins of Hobbs's were at most venial, and the greater part of them were at least a dozen years old. At twenty Hobbs had kissed a girl or two and drunk a glass of beer or two too many. Possibly he had even gone a shade further in both directions, but only a shade. As a boy he had stolen from his hardworking mother's purse, and once he had stolen a doughnut in a baker's shop. But Hobbs was utterly convinced that his childhood and youth had been one long orgy of sin, meriting eternal damnation a dozen times over; at thirty-two he was still paying for them in penance and submission to a God who might some day forgive and who meanwhile only deigned to acknowledge the sinner's existence in such places as the shaft tunnel.

When he had gone the rounds of his eight bearings and seen that they were all properly lubricated, and after he had tried the bilge and made certain water was not rising in the ship, Hobbs took off the little black skull-cap he wore on duty to cushion the blows his head was always sustaining in the tunnel when the ship rolled. He clasped his hands before him – his head was already bowed, thanks to the lowness of the tunnel – and he prayed once more to God for forgiveness for what had passed between him and Mary Walsh that evening in the darkened cinema.

The second hit on *Artemis* did not extinguish the lights in the shaft tunnel immediately. Hobbs felt it and heard it, but it was fifteen seconds later before the flames burned through the insulation of the wiring somewhere along its course and plunged the tunnel into complete darkness. Hobbs stood quite still, hunched over in the tunnel, with no glimmer of light at all. The shaft went on singing its vast song, and all about him was God. He was not afraid. 'X' turret guns above his head fell silent – he could distinguish between a full broadside and the fire merely of 'A' and 'B' turrets – but the framework of the ship transmitted a great many new noises to him, crashes and thumps and bangs, as the flames roared through the stern and the damage control party fought them down. He waited a while for the lights to come on again, but the fire was so far aft that the emergency circuit to the shaft tunnel was involved as well; there would be no more light in the shaft tunnel until – if *Artemis* ever came out of this battle – the wiremen could, under the instructions of the Torpedo Gunner's Mate, restore the circuit. Hobbs took his electric torch out of the pocket of his dungarees and made the round of the bearings again, turning the valves on and off, and when he finished he switched the torch off again. If there was no light there was no light, and that was an end to the business. He certainly was not going to waste the electricity in his torch, for no one – except God who shared the darkness with him – knew how long this action was going to last and how long it would be before he was relieved. God was all about him in the shaft tunnel. He could stand there, bent half double, and wait.

One moment he was alone with God in the darkness of the tunnel; the next, it seemed to him, and he was knee deep in water, so suddenly it poured in. The surprising thing about that water was that it was *hot*. It had not come in direct from the sea – it was sea-water which had been pumped on the flames, had quenched areas of red-hot steel plating, and had thence found its way by devious routes – a fragile light cruiser after two heavy hits and two fires was likely to have many passages open in it – down into the shaft tunnel. As the ship rolled and pitched the water surged up and down the tunnel, almost carrying Hobbs off his feet and splashing up into his face when it broke against the obstacle of his body.

He groped his way through the darkness to the telephone and lifted the receiver. It was some seconds before Howlett or Grant at the telephone switchboard were able to attend to the red light which glowed at the foot of the board to show that the hardly-used telephone in the shaft tunnel was off its hook. During that interval the water rose suddenly again to Hobbs's waist – not hot this time but icy cold, for the red-hot plating was all quenched by now. When the ship rolled the water surged clear over Hobbs's head, throwing him down still holding the receiver. Howlett plugged in – Hobbs heard the welcome click – and said 'Exchange'.

'Engine-room,' said Hobbs, and when he heard the answer, 'Hobbs – shaft tunnel here. I want the officer of the watch.'

The water dashed him against the tunnel walls as he waited again until Lieutenant Bastwick answered him and he made his report.

'We'll pump you out,' said Bastwick. 'Open up the discharge valves.'

Hobbs put back the telephone – under water – and felt his way to the valves. The motion of the ship sent the water up and down the tunnel; not merely did it wash over Hobbs's head, but when his head was clear it also compressed or rarefied the air at the end of the tunnel where Hobbs was so that his eardrums crackled and his breath laboured on those occasions when he had the chance to breathe. The water still flooded into the tunnel – overhead where the damage control party fought the flames it naturally occurred to no one that down in the shaft tunnel their efforts were fast drowning one of their shipmates – and there were twenty tons of it now, hurtling from end to end and from side to side. It picked Hobbs up and dashed him against the water-tight door; the point of his shoulder took the shock, and he felt his collarbone break. It was painful to raise his right arm after that, but he stuck his hand into the front of his dungarees as a substitute sling. The discharge valves were open now, and he hoped the pumps were at work.

The next rush of water up the tunnel was less violent, although it jarred him against the water-tight door and hurt his collarbone again, and the next one was weaker still, hardly over his waist. There were pumps at work all over the ship – some pumping water in as fast as possible to quench the fire, and others pumping it out again as fast as possible from those compartments down into which it drained in torrents, for water-tight doors and water-tight hatchways work only moderately well after a ship has been struck by heavy shells and has had a bad fire rage through a quarter of her length. Hundreds of horse-power were being consumed in this effort, and for hours now the engine-room had been called upon to supply the sixty-five thousand horse-power needed for full speed. The Commander (E) had had the responsibility of seeing to it that engines and boilers would produce more power than they had been designed to produce, and for a longer time than it was fair that they should be asked to do so: the fact that First Class Stoker Hobbs was not drowned miserably in the shaft tunnel was some measure of the Commander (E)'s success in his task.

Hobbs was still alive. His right hand was thrust into the breast of his dungarees, and his shoulder pained him. He was utterly in the dark, for his saturated electric torch refused to function. But he was alive, and he knew his way about the shaft tunnel, from one bearing to another, to the oil valves and back again, and his work which could be carried out one-handed. These were not circumstances in which he felt himself to be justified in asking for relief, and he made no such request; indeed, it did not occur to himself to do so. God was with him in the darkness, and as it happened Hobbs had never been in the shaft tunnel in darkness before. It seemed to him as if in the darkness God was not as implacable, as remorseless, as he was when the tunnel was lit up – that may easily be explained by the harsh black-and-white lighting of the tunnel, for there were no soft tones about it when the bulbs functioned. Very deep down within him, very faintly, Hobbs may have felt that this experience, this being flung about by tons of water in a confined space, his broken collarbone and his near-drowning, was an expiation of his goings-on with Mary Walsh, but Hobbs was a man of slow mental reactions and of morbidly sensitive conscience, and if this feeling was there at all it was very slight, even if later, after mature consideration, it grew stronger. It was just the solid darkness which was comforting to Hobbs, and his reaction to it was to feel as if God were not quite so angry with him. He felt his way round the eight bearings with his left hand, and as he did so he whistled between his teeth, which he had not done since first the conviction of sin had come upon him. It was a very faint little whistle, not audible at all through the high-pitched song of the shaft, and when Hobbs realized what he was doing he cut himself off, but not very abruptly.

24

From the Captain's Report
. . . but firing was maintained . . .

At some time during the few minutes – during the interval measured perhaps in seconds – following immediately after the launching of their torpedoes by the destroyers, a shell was fired from HMS *Artemis* which changed the face of the war, altered the whole history of the world. Men and women in Nigeria or Czechoslovakia would feel the impact of that shell upon their lives. Head-hunting cannibals in Papua, Siberian nomads seeking a scant living among the frozen tundra of Asia, toddling babies in the cornfields of Iowa, and their children's children, would all, in the years to come, owe something to that shell.

For the correct apportionment of the credit the history of that shell and the charge which sent it on its way should be traced back to their origins. There were, somewhere in England, women whose skin was stained yellow by the picric acid which entered into the composition of the bursting charge, who sacrificed strength and beauty in the munitions factory that filled that shell; their hair was bound under caps and their feet encased in felt slippers lest the treacherous material they handled should explode prematurely. There were women at the precision lathes who turned that shell until it fitted exactly, to the thousandth of an inch, into the rifling of the gun that fired it. There were the men that mined the iron and the coal, and the slaving foundry workers who helped to cast the shell. There were the devoted sailors of the Mercantile Marine, who manned the ship that bore the nickel that hardened the steel from Canada to England, in the teeth of the fiercest blockade Germany could maintain. There were the metallurgists who devised the formula for the steel, and there were the chemists who worked upon the explosive. There were the railwaymen and the dockyard workers who handled the deadly thing under the attack of the whole strength of the Nazi air power. The origins of that shell spread too far back and too widely to be traced – forty millions of people made their contribution and their sacrifice that that shell might be fired, forty millions of people whose dead lay in their streets and whose houses blazed round them, working together in the greatest resurgence of patriotism and national spirit that the world has known, a united effort and a united sacrifice which some day may find an historian. Perhaps he will be able to tell of the women and the children and the men who fought for freedom, who gave life and limb, eyesight and health and sanity, for freedom in a long-drawn and unregretted sacrifice.

The miners and the sailors, the munition workers and the railwaymen, had played their part, and now the shell stood in its place in 'A' turret shell-room, and the charge that was to dispatch it lay in its rack in the forward turret magazine. There were only humble workers down there, men like Triggs and Burney who worked in the after-turret magazine. Harbord, the Captain's steward, was stationed in the forward magazine – a thin, dried-up little man, who was aware of the importance of serving bacon and eggs in the most correct manner possible when his Captain called for them. Harbord had come into the Navy from the Reserve, and had passed the earlier years of his life as a steward in the Cunard White Star. He had found promotion there, rising from steward in the second-class to steward in a one-class ship, and from there to steward in the first-class in a slow ship, and eventually supreme promotion, to steward in the first-class in a five-day ship, where the tips were pound notes and five-dollar bills, and where he waited upon film stars and industrial magnates, millionaires and politicians.

He gave them good service; perhaps the best service the world has ever known was that given in the trans-Atlantic luxury liners in the twenties and thirties. He devoted his ingenuity to anticipating the wants of his passengers so that they would be spared even the trouble of asking for what they wanted – he learned to read their characters, sizing them up the first day so that during the next four they would perhaps not have to ask for anything. He could put a basin at the bedside of a seasick millionaire as tactfully as he could serve a midnight supper for two – pork chops and champagne! – in the cabin of a nymphomaniac film star. He was unobtrusive and yet always available. When passengers tried to pump him about their fellow-passengers he could supply what appeared to be inside information without disclosing anything at all. He knew the great, the wealthy, and the notorious, in their weakest moments, and to him they were not in the least heroic figures. Yet of his feelings he gave no sign; he was deferential without being subservient, helpful without being fulsome.

The trade agreement between the shipping lines regulated the fares charged so that the only way in which they could compete with each other was in the services they could offer – menus ten pages long, food from every quarter of the globe, masterpieces of art hanging on the bulkheads, orchestras and gymnasiums and swimming baths; the concerted efforts of ingenious minds were at work devising fresh ways of pampering the first-class passengers so that a thousand miles from land they were surrounded by luxuries of which Nero or Lucullus never dreamed, by comforts such as Queen Victoria never enjoyed. And the service which the stewards could give was an important part of this system. If by a particular manner and bearing Harbord could make his charges more comfortable, he was ready to display that manner and bearing – it was his job for the moment. The social system which permitted – encouraged – such luxury and waste, and which made him the servant of drunken ne'er-do-wells and shifty politicians was obviously in need of reform, but the reformation must start with the system, not with the symptoms. Meanwhile he had work to do, and Harbord took pride in doing to the best of his ability the work which was to be done.

And when war came and the Navy claimed his services it was far easier to reconcile his prejudices with the type of work to which he was allotted. He was a steward, still, but the Captain's steward – trust the

Captain to select the best available. The arts he had acquired in the Cunard White Star were of real use now, to serve a breakfast without breaking in on the Captain's train of thought, to attend to the trivial and mechanical details of the Captain's day so that it was only the war which made demands upon the Captain's reserves of mental energy. At sea when the Captain was day and night on the bridge, it was Harbord's duty to keep him well fed and well clad, and in port Harbord had to shield him from nervous irritation so as to allow him a chance to recuperate. His discretion and his trustworthiness were of real value nowadays; the desk in the Captain's cabin held papers which the German staff would gladly pay a million pounds to see – Harbord never allowed his mind to record the writing which his eyes rested upon. Visitors came to the Captain's cabin, officers of the ship, officers of other ships, Intelligence officers of the Army and Air Force Staffs, Admirals and Generals.

They talked freely with the Captain, and Harbord in his pantry or offering sherry and pink gin from a tray could hear all they said. Sometimes it would be things that would make the spiciest shipboard gossip – news as to where the ship was going, or alterations in routine, or promotions, or transfers, or arrangements for shore leave. Sometimes it would be matters of high policy, the course of the naval war, the tactics to be employed in the next battle, or the observed effects of new weapons or new methods. Sometimes it would merely be reminiscence, tales of battle with submarine or aeroplane or armed raider. Whatever it was, it was bound to be of the most engrossing interest. An advance word to the lower deck on the subject of leave would make his confidants his grateful clients; when talking to his friends on shore Harbord could have been most gratifyingly pontifical about the progress of the war; and in every port there lurked men and women who would pay anything in money and kind for news of how such-and-such a submarine was sunk or what happened to such-and-such a raider. But Harbord was deaf and dumb and blind, just as he had been in peacetime when the newspaper reporters had tried to find out from him who it was who shared the politician's cabin at night.

When the hands went to action stations his was a position of no such responsibility. He was like Triggs, merely a man who stripped the tin cover from the cordite charges and thrust the cardboard-cased cylinders of explosive through the flash-tight shutter of the magazine into the handling-room – his duties about the Captain allowed neither the time nor the opportunity to train him to do more responsible work. He was hardly aware of his unimportance; that much effect, at least, his previous experience had had on him. He handed the cordite with as much solemnity as when he offered sherry to a Vice-Admiral, although with a greater rapidity of movement. A lifetime of self-control had left him with little surface light-heartedness, just as the habitual guard he maintained over his tongue made the men who worked beside him think him surly and unfriendly. At his action station he was in close contact with half a dozen men, because 'A' and 'B' magazines were combined into one, with a flash-tight shutter both forward and aft, the one opening into 'A' turret handling-room and the other into 'B'. During the periods of idleness when the guns were not firing the men could stand about and gossip, all except Harbord, who would not. His fellow workers – the queerest mixture, from Clay, the ship's painter, to Sutton of the canteen staff – had, as a result of their different employments, the most varied gossip to exchange, and Harbord's could have been a valued contribution. But he kept his mouth shut, and was repaid by his shipmates saying he put on all the airs of an admiral. Of all these it was Harbord who was privileged to be the man who handled the propellant charge that sent to its target the shell that changed history.

Forward in the shell-room it was Able Seaman Colquhoun who handled the shell – a big curly-haired young giant from Birkenhead, whose worst cross in life was the tendency of the uninitiated to mispronounce his name and give the 'l' and 'q' their full value. It was always a ticklish job telling petty officers that he called himself 'Ca-hoon'; self-important petty officers were inclined to look on that as an impertinence. The six-inch shell that Colquhoun handled weighed one hundred pounds, which was why his youthful thews and sinews were employed here in the shell-room. In a rolling ship it called for a powerful man to heave as big a weight as that with certainty into the hoist.

Colquhoun was proud of his strength, and to put it to good use gratified some instinct within him. He smiled reminiscently as he bent and heaved. In the early days of the black-out in England, when his ship was under orders to sail, he had spent his last night's leave ashore with Lily Ford, the big blonde friend of his boyhood, who had repelled every advance made to her by every man she had met. She had kept her virginity as though it were a prize in a competition, not selfishly, not prudishly, but as if she looked on herself as if she were as good as any man and would not yield until she should meet one whom she could admit to be her better. But that night on the canal bank, under the bright moon of the first September of the war, Colquhoun had put out all his strength. It had been careless of Lily to let herself be lured by Colquhoun's tact to such a deserted spot as the canal bank, but it would really have been the same if there had been help within call – Lily would not have called for help to deal with a situation she could not deal with single-handed. She fought with him, silently, desperately, at first, and even when he was pressing her hard she would not do more than whisper hoarsely, 'Get away, you beast.' She writhed and struggled, putting out all the strength of her tough body, trained by the factory labours which had given her her glorious independence. Then she yielded to his overpowering force, breaking down suddenly and completely, her savage words trailing off into something between a sigh and a sob, her stiff body relaxing into submission, the mouth she had kept averted seeking out his in the darkness.

It was a succulent memory for the graceless Colquhoun something to be rolled over the tongue of reminiscence, every detail just as it should have been, even to the walk back from the canal bank with Lily clinging to him, her boasted self-sufficiency all evaporated, and the fact that Colquhoun's ship was under orders to sail terrifying in its imminence and inevitability. She had clung and she had even wept, although the day before she would have laughed at any suggestion that she would waste a tear on any man.

Well, that was two and a half years ago, and it was to be presumed that she had got over it by now.

'Come up, you bastard!' said Colquhoun without ill temper, for he was still grinning to himself; the arms that had clasped Lily Ford clasped the shell that was to change history, and slid it forward into the hoist.

At the same moment in the handling-room Able Seaman Day, the man who lost his left forefinger as a result of a premature explosion at the battle of the River Plate, took the charge that Harbord had thrust through the flash-tight shutter and pushed it into a pocket on the endless chain that ran up above his head through another flash-tight hatchway. The hoist rose, the endless chain revolved, the shell and charge arrived simultaneously in 'A' turret lobby.

The designer of a ship of war encounters difficulties at every turn. One school of naval thought clamours for guns, the largest possible guns in the greatest possible number, with which an enemy may be overwhelmed without the opportunity of hitting back. Another school demands speed, and points out that the best guns in the world are useless unless they can be carried fast enough to catch the enemy. A third school prudently calls for armour because, as Nelson once pointed out, a battle at sea is the most uncertain of all conflicts, and speed and guns may vanish in a fiery holocaust as a result of a single hit. And armour means weight, and guns mean weight, the one at the expense of the other and both at the expense of the weight that can be allotted to engines.

The designer reaches a compromise with these conflicting demands only to come against new incompatibles. Men must be able to live in a ship; the mere processes of living demand that they should be able to go from one part of the ship to another, and when she is in action it may well be that they have to do so with the greatest possible speed. But, once again, she may be struck by shells or bombs or torpedoes, and to minimize the damage of the hit she must be divided up into the greatest possible number of compartments bulkheaded off from each other, and those bulkheads must be free of all openings – except that there is the most urgent need for wires and voice pipes and ventilating shafts to pass through them.

In the same way the gunnery expert insists that his guns should be placed as high as possible, so as to give the greatest possible command, and his insistence is met with the reply that guns and gun-mountings are the heaviest things in a ship and putting them high up means imperilling the ship's stability like standing up in a rowing boat. Not merely that, but the gunnery expert, wise to the danger of high explosives, demands that although his guns should be as high above the level of the sea as possible the shells and the charges for the guns should be out of harm's way and as far below that level as possible; then, unreasonable as a spoilt child, he goes on to clamour for guns that will fire with the greatest rapidity and in consequence needing to be supplied every minute with a great weight of ammunition regardless of the distance it must be raised from shell-room and magazine. Even that is not all. The moment his wishes appear to be granted he baulks at the thought of a long chain of high explosive extending unbroken from top to bottom of the ship, and he insists that the chain be broken up and interrupted with flash-tight hatchways and shutters that must on no account delay the passage of the ammunition from the magazine to the precious guns.

Ingenious mechanisms solve this problem – so that when 'X' turret lobby in *Artemis* was set on fire the flames did not flash up into the turret nor down into the magazine – and then the designer is faced with a new difficulty, because the turret must, of course, be able to revolve, to turn from side to side, so that the belts and hoists are attached at one end to the stationary lobby, and at the other to the revolving turret; and this is the difficulty which designers for eighty years have struggled against. When Ericsson built *Monitor* he had a hole cut in the floor of the turret and another in the roof of the magazine below, and in order for ammunition to be passed up the turret had to be revolved until the two holes corresponded and the turret had to remain stationary until it was re-ammunitioned – a state of affairs no gunnery officer, intent on annihilating the enemy, would tolerate for a moment.

Even the apparently insoluble problem of the revolving turret and the stationary lobby has been solved now, so that whichever way the turret may be turning two shells of a hundred pounds each and two charges of cordite arrive in it every ten seconds to feed the guns, but the complication has forced another compromise upon the unfortunate designer. He is faced by the choice between employing men or machines – elaborate, complicated machines which may be disabled by a hit, or men who have to be fed, and given water to drink, and somewhere to sling a hammock, and who, in a nation exerting the last ounce of its strength, could be employed on some other urgent duty if not engaged in manhandling ammunition. Faced by this choice, the designer compromises, as he has compromised in his designs all through the ship. He makes the mechanisms as simple as he can without necessitating too great use of manpower, and he cuts down his manpower as far as he can without complicating the mechanisms too much. He ends, of course, by satisfying neither the Commander who is responsible for the men's living conditions nor the Gunnery Officer who is responsible for the guns, but that is the natural fate of designers of ships – the speed enthusiasts and the gunnery experts and the advocates of armour protection, the men who have to keep the ships at sea and the men who have to handle them in action all combine to curse the designer. Then comes the day of battle, and the mass of compromises which is a ship of war encounters another ship of war which is a mass of different compromises, and then, ten to one, the fighting men on the winning side will take all the credit to themselves and the losers – such of them as survive – will blame the designer all over again.

So the thews and sinews of Able Seaman Colquhoun and the fussy diligence of Harbord were necessary to start the shell and its propelling charge on the way up from shell-room and magazine to 'A' turret lobby. Then Able Seaman Mobbs tipped the shell out of the hoist into the shell ring; to him it was just one more shell, and not the shell on which the destinies of the world depended. With one shell arriving up the hoist every five seconds he had no time for profound thought. He had to be as diligent as a beaver, and he was a man of full body, oddly enough. The stooping and the heaving which he had to do in the warm atmosphere of the lobby had no apparent effect on the waistline which week by week grew a little more salient as Mobbs left youth farther behind and advanced further into maturity. He swept the sweat from his forehead with the back of his right forearm, avoiding the use of his hands, which were filthy from contact with the shells. But by now his forearm was nearly as dirty as his hands, and the sweat and the dirt combined into fantastic streaks diagonally across his pink face. On his cheeks and chin there was a fuzz of fair beard like a chicken's down, for Mobbs had been carried away early in the war by the revived Naval craze for beards, and the poverty of the result had not yet induced him to reapply for permission to shave. The fuzz was dirty in patches, too, and there were little rivers of sweat running through it. Anyone in the lobby with leisure for thought would have smiled at the sight of him, his plethoric pink face and his ridiculous beard, his blue pop-eyes as innocent as a child's, and the streaked dirt over all. He moved the shell ring round for a quarter of a revolution to where Ordinary Seaman Fiddler awaited it, and then he brushed his face with his left forearm and managed to streak it again in the diagonally opposite direction, thereby giving the finishing touch to his ludicrous appearance. No one had time to notice it, however. Another shell had come up the hoist, dispatched by Able Seaman Colquhoun, and he had to deal with it – just another shell, no different in its appearance from its important predecessor now under the charge of Ordinary Seaman Fiddler, no different from the scores that had gone before, or from the scores which, for all Mobbs knew, would follow after. It seemed to him as if he had been at work for hours tipping shells from hoist to ring and would go on doing so to the end of time. The thunder of the guns just above his head, the motion of the ship, made no impression on him; for that matter he was not even actively conscious of the stuffy heat of the lobby. Word had come through over the telephone system that 'X' turret lobby had been wiped out, and after magazine flooded, 'X' turret guns silenced. Mobbs heard the news as he toiled and sweated; some of his messmates were gone, and it must have been only by a miracle that he and *Artemis* together had escaped being blown into microscopic fragments. None of that was as important as this business of keeping the shell ring full and the hoist empty, not as important at the moment, at least.

Meanwhile Ordinary Seaman Filmore took from the endless chain the cordite charge that Harbord below him had put into it, and transferred it to the cordite hoist of the revolving structure – three neat movements did it all, in far less than the five seconds allowed him. It was an easy job for Filmore. He had time to think and talk. The empty pocket in the endless chain flicked out of sight through the flash-tight hatchway.

'Coo!' said Filmore. 'That means old Nobby's gone. *You* know. Not Nobby the Leading Cook. The other one wiv the red 'air. 'E owes me a couple o' pints, too. Last time –'

'Shut up,' snapped Petty Officer Ransome.

He should not have snapped; he should have given the order naturally and easily, as orders which must be obeyed under pain of death should be given, and he was conscious of his error the moment the words were out of his mouth. But he was newly promoted and not quite sure of himself, and the responsibility of 'A' turret lobby weighed heavily on him.

'Keep yer 'air on!' said Filmore to himself, very careful that he should not be overheard. By diligent testing he knew just how far he could go with every Petty Officer and Leading Seaman in the ship. He had the Cockney quick wit, and the Cockney interest in disaster and death. He felt about the death of the red-haired Nobby Clark in the same way as his mother in her Woolwich slum felt about the death of a neighbour. It was a most interesting event; although the daily miracles of sunrise and sunset quite failed to impress him, he was always struck by the miracle that someone he knew, had talked to and talked about, should now be something quite different, a mere lump of flesh destined to immediate mouldering and decay. It was not intrinsically a morbid interest, and certainly the death of Nobby Clark was something to be talked about, like a birth in the Royal family. Petty Officer Ransome thought otherwise. If he had been a mere seaman he would gladly have entered into the discussion, recalling old memories of Nobby, and wondering how his widow would get along on her pension. But as a Petty Officer, responsible for 'A' turret lobby, and with an unjustified fear that it was bad for the morale of the men to dwell on the death of a shipmate, he cut the discussion short. As a distraction he gave another order.

'Keep it moving, Fiddler.'

'Aye, aye,' said Fiddler.

The shell vanished into the hoist in the revolving

structure as a fresh broadside blared overhead. Ransome, in this his first action as a Petty Officer, was worried. From the time of going to action stations he had felt a nagging fear lest his lobby should not be as efficient as the other two, lest a broadside should be delayed because ammunition was supplied more slowly to 'A' turret than to 'B' and 'X'. If that should happen there would be a sharp reprimand from Sub-Lieutenant Coxe over his head; even worse, the Gunnery Lieutenant, watching the 'gun ready' lamps, might – certainly would – be moved to inquire into the cause of the delay. It was not fear of actual reprimand, or of punishment or disrating, which Ransome felt, any more than the crew of a racing eight fears defeat as it waits at the starting point. It was mere nervousness, which sharpened his voice and led him into giving unnecessary orders, and it remained to be seen if time and experience would enable him to overcome this weakness. No man's capacity for command can be known until it has been tried in actual battle.

In point of fact, 'A' turret was easier to keep supplied than 'B' turret just aft of it. 'B' turret was superimposed, raised higher above the deck than 'A', so as to enable its guns, when pointed directly forward, to fire over it. Yet 'A' and 'B' turrets drew their ammunition from the same magazine, and from shell rooms at the same level below the sea, with the result that 'B's' shells and charges had to be sent up on a journey a full seven feet longer that 'A's', enough to make an appreciable difference in the time of transmission and to demand a proportionate increase in efficiency on the part of 'B's' turret crew. Since his promotion Ransome had not begun to reason this out and comfort himself with the knowledge, which was a pity, for when nervousness begins to reason it ceases to be nervousness. Instead, he snapped, 'Keep it moving, Fiddler,' quite unnecessarily.

'Aye aye,' grumbled Fiddler, a little resentfully, for he knew that there was nothing slow about his supervision of the shell ring. He was an old, old sailor who had seen Petty Officers come and Petty Officers go, who had been through battle and shipwreck and hardship and pestilence, sturdily refusing promotion despite the recommendations of Lieutenants and the suggestions of Commanders. The life of an Able Seaman was a comfortable one, a satisfactory one, and he did not want the even tenor of his existence broken by the responsibilities of promotion. He did not look upon his experiences when the destroyer *Apache* was lost in a snowstorm in the Hebrides, and he had clung to a ledge of a cliff for a night and half a day with the waves beating just below him, as an interruption of his placid existence, nor the fighting at Narvik, nor the week he spent in an open boat when his sloop was torpedoed. Those were mere incidents, but to be even a Leading Seaman meant disturbing all the comfortable habits and daily routine acquired during twenty years of service. All he wanted to do was to go steadily along performing the duties allotted him, gaining neither credit nor discredit, neither promotion nor punishment, but reserving to himself the right to feel that he knew much more about seamanship and gunnery than did these whippersnapper young Petty Officers whom they promoted nowadays. Ransome's order to him called forth the mechanical response to his lips, but did not quicken his movements in the least, for he knew he was doing his job perfectly, and probably a great deal better than Ransome could. The shell slid under his guidance from the shell ring to the revolving hoist, and soared up to the turret and out of his life, keeping pace as before with the cordite charge in the cordite hoist.

Sub-Lieutenant Coxe allowed his eyes to rest idly on the shell as it lay in its trough on its arrival, with its ugly distinctive paint on it, and ugly in its harsh cylindro-conical outline. There was not even a functional beauty about it, unlike most of the weapons of war, nor was it large enough to be impressive in its bulk. A six-inch shell, even one which is destined to free humanity, is unredeemingly ugly. Coxe never stopped to think for a moment whether it was ugly or beautiful. He was keeping a sharp eye on his guns' crews, watching each of their intricate movements. Coxe knew all about this turret and the principles that it embodied. He knew all the details of its mechanism, all the bolts and all the levers. If every six-inch turret in the Royal Navy, and every blue-print and every working drawing were to be destroyed in some unheard-of cataclysm, they could be replaced by reference to Sub-Lieutenant Coxe. When he was sea-sick (which was often) Coxe could forget his troubles by closing his eyes and calling up before him the obturator on the vent axial bolt or the tapered grooves in the recoil cylinder, but there was no need for sea-sickness to set him thinking about gunnery. It occupied most of his thoughts; and in the same way that a man at dinner turns satisfied from a joint to complete the meal with cheese, so Coxe could turn from the comparatively simple mechanics of the gun-mountings to the mathematics of ballistics, and Henderson and Hasse's differential form of Resal's fundamental equation.

Coxe was an example of the mathematical prodigy, as his first-class certificates showed; at twenty his facility in the subject was striking. The fact that England was at war was at least postponing his specializing; a prolonged period of peace would almost inevitably have resulted in his being confined to desk work in a state of voluntary servitude, hugging his chains, respected, perhaps, in his own speciality, but unknown beyond a limited circle. In those conditions he would have been likely to forget that war is not a clash of mathematical formulae, but a contest waged by men of flesh and blood and brain. If anything would help to keep him human, to develop him into a wise leader of men instead of into a learned computer, it was his present command, where under his own eye he could see formulae and machinery and men in action together. The proving ground and the testing station could confirm or destroy theories about internal pressures and the toughness of armour plate, but only the proving ground of war could test men. The most beautiful machines, the most elaborate devices, were useless if the men who handled them were badly trained or shaken by fear, and there was the interesting point that the more complex the machinery, and the more human effort it saved, and the more exactly it performed its functions, the greater need there was for heroes to handle it. Not mere individual heroes either, but a whole team of heroes. Disaster would be the result of a weak link anywhere along the long chain of the ship's organization. A frightened rangetaker, a jumpy Marine bandsman at the Transmitting Station table, a shaken steward in the magazine, and all the elaborate mechanism, the marvellous optical instruments, the cannons that cost a king's ransom, and the machine which embodied the ingenuity of generations, were all of them useless. It would be better then if there had never been any development in gunnery, and they were still in the days when the gunnery handbook made use of the elastic expression, 'take about a shovelful of powder'. Euclid had pointed out that the whole is equal to the sum of all its parts, and it was dawning upon Coxe that there was not merely a mathematical application of that axiom.

With a new eye he saw Numbers Four and Five ram home the shell into the left-hand gun; he was familiar with the very abstruse mathematics involved in calculations regarding compensation for wear at the breech of the gun, and those calculations always assumed that the projectile would be firmly seated against the rifling. Some dry-as-dust individual at Woolwich made those calculations, some withered officer with rings on his sleeve and gold oak-leaves on his cap brim, but unless Number Five, there, the hairy individual with the crossed flags of England and France tattooed on his forearms, kept his head and wielded the rammer efficiently, those calculations might as well never have been put on paper.

Number Six was pushing in the charge. It had never occurred to Coxe before that the instructions which ordered this were no guarantee that it would be done. Number Six might drop the charge, or if his hands were shaking or he was not seaman enough to keep his footing, he might break it open against the sharp edge. Number Six might even become frightened enough to dash out of the turret and run below to take shelter under the main deck – that was a possibility that had never crossed Coxe's mind before, he realized, and yet it was a possibility. Number Six had a tendency to boils on the back of his neck; Coxe had never noticed that before either, but a man who could suffer from boils was a man and not a piece of machinery that shoved the propellant up the breech. Number Six – what the devil was his name? Stokes? Something like that. No, it was Merivale, of course – Number Six was a fallible human being. Coxe became guiltily conscious that it was even conceivable that Number Six would be less likely to run away when he should be pushing in charges if the officer of the quarters did not call him Stokes when his name was Merivale. That was not something that could be reduced to a mathematical formula. It was courage, morale, *esprit de corps*, discipline – of a sudden these were pregnant words for Coxe now.

He turned with a fresh interest to Number Two, who was closing the breech. Coxe was nearly sure that Number Two's name was Hammond. He really must make an effort to remember. Hammond – if that was his name – was having trouble with his wife. The matter had come up when the Commander was interviewing request-men. Some neighbour, officious or well-intentioned or spiteful or over-moral, had written to Hammond telling him about nocturnal visitors to Hammond's home. White-faced and sick with despair, on the sunny quarterdeck, Hammond had admitted to the Commander that he would not be surprised if the accusation were true. 'She was like that,' said Hammond. Once she had promised that it would never occur again, and Hammond had believed her, but standing before the Commander, Hammond had reluctantly admitted that he had been an optimistic fool; yet clearly that had not made it easier for Hammond, his life in ruins, and only half-hearted even now in his desire to cut off his allotment of pay to the wife he was still, obviously, besotted about.

A man whose wife was being unfaithful to him was liable to neglect his business. Coxe was academically aware of that even though he could not conceive of anything, certainly not domestic unhappiness, coming between him and gunnery. He darted a glance to see that Hammond had inserted the tube and masked the vent. Hammond swung the breech shut and closed the interruptor.

'Ready!' he said quietly – Number Two at the other gun shouted the word excitedly. Hammond was cool; cold might be a better word for it. It might be merely the deadly coldness of an embittered man; but, on the other hand, it might be the effect of discipline and training. Coxe actually found himself wondering which it was.

Shell and charge were in the gun now. Magazine and shell-room and handing-room, lobby and turret, had all made their contribution. So had every man in the ship, from Hobbs down in the shaft tunnel to the Captain on the bridge and Whipple at the masthead. The fact that the shell now lying in the breech of the left-hand gun 'A' turret was going assuredly to alter the history of the world was something to the credit of every one of them. The whole is equal to the sum of all its parts.

'Shoot!' said the Gunnery Lieutenant for the hundredth time that day. His fighting blood was still roused; the long battle had not brought weariness or lassitude. He controlled and directed this broadside as thoroughly as he had controlled the first.

The elevation and deflection of the guns was fixed by the Transmitting Station; this broadside meant no more and no less to the men there than any other in the long fight. The Marine bandsmen followed their pointers and Mr Kaile handled his complex orchestra as always, and the fire gong rang for the hundredth time in the Transmitting Station as Chief Petty Officer O'Flaherty in the Director Control Tower obeyed the Gunnery Lieutenant's order and pressed the trigger, to fire the broadside that would decide the future of neutral Ireland just as much as that of the rest of the belligerent world. The tubes heated, the charges exploded, and the four shells went shrieking over nine thousand yards of sea to their destined ends. Three of them missed, and the fourth one – the shell from the left-hand gun in 'A' turret – hit. The spotters in *Artemis* recorded 'straddle' and set themselves in ignorance of what that straddle meant to observe the next fall of shot.

25

From the Captain's Report

. . . until the enemy turned away . . .

Kapitän-sur-see Helmuth von Bödicke stood on the signal bridge of His Italian Majesty's battleship *Legnano* with Vice-Ammiráglio Gasparo Gaetano Nocentini. They were out of earshot of their staffs, who stood decently back so as not to overhear the conversation of the two great men, who were talking French to each other; only when French failed them did they turn and summon Korvetten Kápitan Klein and Luogotenènte Lorenzetti to translate for them from German into Italian and from Italian into German. At the time when von Bödicke was young enough to learn languages it never occurred to any German naval officer that it might some day be specially useful to speak Italian, and Nocentini had learned French in the nursery and had never had either the desire or the intention to acquire the language of the barbarians of the north.

The signal bridge in *Legnano* was windy and exposed, but it was the most convenient place in the ship for the commanding admiral; the conning tower was too crowded and its view too limited, while the signal bridge afforded the most rapid means of communication with the rest of the fleet. On the port side where Bödicke and Nocentini stood they had the best view of whatever was visible. Abeam of them was the immensely long black smudge of the smoke screen which the English had laid down, and against that background, vague and shadowy, were the English light cruisers, screened from view during much of the time by the splashes thrown up by the Italian salvoes. Fine on the port bow were the English destroyers, just wheeling round like swallows on the wing, after presumably launching their torpedoes against the Italian line. Astern of *Legnano* came the other Italian ships, the battleship *San Martino*, the heavy cruisers and the light cruisers. What Bödicke and Nocentini could not see from the port side of the signal bridge were the Italian destroyers advancing too late against the English destroyers, but as they undoubtedly were too late it did not matter so much that they could not be seen.

The din that assailed the ears of the men on the signal bridge was enormous, frightful. Every twenty-five seconds the fifteen-inch guns let loose a salvo louder than the loudest thunderclap, whose tremendous detonation shook them like a violent blow, and, deep-toned behind them, *San Martino*'s big guns echoed those salvoes. These were intermittent noises; the din of the secondary armament went on without cessation, six-inch and four-inch and twelve-pounder all banging away as fast as they could be loaded and fired in the endeavour to beat back the destroyer attack. It was ear-splitting and made it hard to think clearly. And all round the ship were raining the broadsides from the English light cruiser, deluging the decks with splashes, or bursting against the armour with a piercing crash, straddling the ship so closely that the shells that passed overhead were audible through the detonations of the secondary armament.

Von Bödicke trained his glasses on the leading English cruiser. She was badly on fire aft, with thick smoke pouring out of her, and yet she was still firing superbly and fast. The rest of the line appeared to have suffered little damage, which was quite absurd seeing how much they had been under fire. These excitable Italians could never steady themselves quickly enough to hit an elusive target. Brave enough men, perhaps (presumably because of the infiltration of Nordic blood into their Mediterranean veins), but unsteady. He experienced a momentary feeling of helplessness when he thought of his mission; he had been sent here to crush the British fleet by the aid of the Italian, and now he was conscious of the weakness of the tool he had to employ. He was like a man setting out to move a heavy rock and finding his crowbar buckling in his hand.

He let his glasses hang by their cord from his neck, and he plucked at the torpedo beard he wore as a tribute to the memory of von Hipper. Naval warfare, a naval battle, was like a game of poker. A good hand was of no avail if it met a better; confronted with four of a kind a full house was as unprofitable as a pair of deuces; the winner scooped the pool and the loser had nothing. In land warfare, or in air warfare, the loser might hope for a profitable defeat, to gain so much time or to inflict so much loss as to nullify the other's victory, but at sea it was all or nothing.

It was all or nothing for him, von Bödicke, as well. Von Bödicke remembered receiving supplementary verbal orders at the Marineamt, and the thin lips and the almost colourless eyes of Admiral Fricke, the Chief of the Naval Staff. He could expect no mercy from Fricke if he were to fail, and it was no comfort to think that Fricke could expect no mercy either. Fricke was primarily a Nazi and only secondarily a naval officer, who had won his position through all the clashes and fierce jealousies of the Party. If the command of the Mediterranean were not achieved other ambitious young men would pull Fricke down. And Fricke would die, of heart diesase or a motoring accident, for a man who tried for power by way of the Party staked his life on the result; successful rivals would never run the risk of his regaining power and avenging himself, nor would the Führer. The blackguards of the Party acted on the principle that dead men knife no one in the back. Fricke would die, and old von Bödicke would merely be ruined, put on beggarly retired pay under police supervision. He would not even have enough to eat, for he would be a useless mouth, on the lowest scale of rations, and doomed to slow starvation because no one would help a man with no return favours in his gift to supplement his diet illegally. He turned to Nocentini beside him.

'We must turn towards the enemy, your excellency,' he said.

Nocentini looked down at von Bödicke, Nocentini tall and gangling and clean-shaven, von Bödicke short and stocky with a little bristling beard. Nocentini had received verbal instructions as well, and his came direct from the lips of il Duce. Il Duce had been most explicit on the point that nothing was to be risked. An easy victory was to be grasped at eagerly, but only as long as there was no prospect of loss. The battleships with which Nocentini was entrusted were the only ones left serviceable in the Italian navy, and very precious in consequence. Il Duce had far-reaching theories about war; one was that it was most necessary to husband one's strength against the possible demands of an always dangerous future, and the other was that by biding one's time one always found opportunities to pick up highly profitable gains for almost nothing as long as one had not dissipated one's strength prematurely. Il Duce had been most eloquent about this, making his points one after the other with much slapping of his fat white hands on the table while the sweat made his flabby jowls shine in the lamplight. He preached caution in the privacy of his office with just as much fervour as he preached recklessness from his balcony. But the fervour had an unhappy ring, and the arguments were those of a beaten man, of a tired man. Il Duce was growing old.

That was one of the considerations Nocentini had to bear in mind. One of these days il Duce would die, and no one could tell what régime would find itself in power; there might be prolonged chaos. A powerful fleet would be a potent factor in the struggle, and Nocentini had ideas about how to use it. So he was in complete agreement with the Chief of the State about the desirability of easy victories and the necessity to avoid crippling losses. He knew that it was only with the utmost reluctance that il Duce had consented to risking the fleet three hundred miles from its base, even when the Germans, in their usual cocksure fashion, had assured him that the English had no capital ships whatever available in the Eastern Mediterranean. Nocentini fancied that the Germans had been using a great deal of pressure, threatening in the event of a refusal to cut down still further the tiny shipments of coal that just enabled Italian civilization to exist.

If he could wipe out this British squadron and its convoy it would add to his own prestige and that of the fleet, but it would restore something to the prestige of il Duce as well. The wiping out would not be easy, for the English had already shown their readiness to fight to the last. Those early moves of his, cautious feelers to determine the British attitude, had proved this. To turn towards the enemy, to plunge into the smoke screen, would mean a muddled battle, an undignified scuffle, and possibly heavy losses in a close-range action. Nocentini simply did not believe the optimistic reports with which the Naval Intelligence kept bombarding him regarding the extremities to which Malta was reduced. He was not a natural optimist; and with regard to Malta, he had the unhappy suspicion that its fall would be just another chestnut pulled out of the fire for the benefit of the Germans.

Italy? Nocentini was not sure now what Italy was. Not Mussolini, assuredly. The vulgarian who had built up the Italian fleet, who had given it more men and more money than Nocentini had ever dreamed of, had something once to recommend him. But the frightened worn-out man, prematurely old, cowering in the Quirinal, pathetically pleading with Nocentini to be cautious, and with the haunting fear of the Nazis to be read in his face, was not a leader to be followed with devotion, and certainly not the embodiment of the Italy which Nocentini vaguely dreamed about.

The continuous crash of the guns, the constant arrival of reports, the very wind that whipped round their ears, confused Nocentini's mind and made thinking difficult. He stood and gazed down at von Bödicke, wasting precious seconds while the torpedoes were actually on their way towards them.

'Your Excellency,' said von Bödicke 'it is absolutely necessary that you should give the order.'

Von Bödicke was in a desperate mood. He was disillusioned on every side. He suspected a policy of deliberate obstruction. In the opening moves of the battle heavy smoke had poured from the funnels first of this ship and then of that one prematurely revealing the position of the fleet. Any engineer ought to be ashamed of himself for permitting such a thing to happen; the lowest *maschinist-maat* in the German navy would know better. He had goaded Nocentini into signalling reprimands, and the replies that came back had been decidedly unsettling. One captain had blamed the oil fuel, and in the wording of his message had insolently suggested that the fuel's defects were due to the culpable carelessness of the German authorities who had supplied it. The worst of that suggestion was that it was possibly true; von Bödicke knew a little about Albert Speer, who made use of his position as Oil Fuel Controller to make profits for the dummy company which was really Albert Speer. With boiler-room crews as excitable as the Italians, it was too much to expect that they should keep their heads clear enough to deal instantly and accurately with crises like fluctuations in the quality of the oil in the pipes.

These damned Italians were all alike. They were

jumpy and excitable. Most of them had had too little training at sea either to be able to master sea-sickness or to be able to carry out their duties in a crisis with a seaway running. They had been firing away at the cruisers all this time and hardly scored a hit – when the action began he had visited turrets and gunnery control towers, to find officers and men chattering like apes and getting in each other's way. Von Bödicke suspected that half the salvoes they fired off had been unaimed as a result of inefficiency on the part of the guns' crews or the gunnery control crews; it was too much to expect that somewhere along the complicated chain there would not be at least one weak link – especially as the veteran seamen were being drained away from the ships to make good the steady losses in submarine crews.

Von Bödicke's desperation was being eaten away by a growing weariness. He hated Fricke for sending him on this thankless duty. Victory would confirm Fricke in his position; and Bödicke suddenly realized that bloody defeat might do the same. If he, Bödicke, were able to persuade Nocentini to make an attack, and this *Legnano* were to be sunk, and Bödicke along with her, Bödicke having done his best and the Italian navy proved to be obviously not up to its work, then no one could possibly blame Fricke. He would continue to lord it at the Marineamt. Self-pity came to soften von Bödicke's desperations as well. It was a frightful dilemma in which he found himself. This was no simple marine problem which he faced. It was a complex of political and personal factors intricately entangled. With a German fleet under his command, in German waters, he would not hesitate for a moment about what to do, but out here in the Mediterranean with these Italians it was quite different. The very name of the ship in which he found himself was an insult to Germany. Legnano was the name of the battlefield where der Alte Barbarossa had by chance met with defeat at the hands of the Lombard League. Mussolini had no business to recall to memory that unfortunate accident of seven hundred years ago. But it was just like the Italians; when they decided to call their battleships after Italian victories they soon found themselves running out of names. *San Martino* astern was named after a battle which was really an Austrian victory, terminated by an Austrian retreat merely because of the success of the French on the other battlefield of Solferino. At Vittorio Veneto the decisive blow was struck by an English army, and then only after Austria had been stabbed in the back by the Jews and separatists. Von Bödicke remembered the sneer in which German naval officers so often indulged when they asked the rhetorical question why the Italians had named no battleship of theirs after Caporetto. The question was on the tip of his tongue as he looked at Nocentini, so bitter was his mood.

He had asked to have the Italian fleet turned towards the enemy, but he had no sooner said the words when he experienced a revulsion of spirit. He could not recall them, but he was in two minds about it. He simply did not know what he wanted. He was balanced on a knife edge of indecision, and Nocentini, looking down at him, knew it telepathically. He was just as undetermined, just as unsettled in his mind as was Bödicke. The minutest influence would decide him, like Bödicke, one way or the other.

'We must turn either towards or away,' said Nocentini slowly, groping with difficulty, in his dazed preoccupation, for the French words.

He would have liked more time to discuss it, so as to postpone the moment of decision, but he knew that was vain. It was twenty seconds at least since the British destroyers had launched their torpedoes. Nocentini looked over at the British squadron, at the smoke-wreathed silhouettes aflame with gun flashes. He knew much about the British Navy, and in that clairvoyant moment he visualized the disciplined sailors bending to their work, the shells quietly passed up from the magazine, the rapid loading and the accurate firing. And at that moment there was flung into the scale that factor that tipped it down and swayed the balance of von Bödicke's and Nocentini's hesitating minds. A six-inch shell struck full upon 'B' turret, below them and forward of them, and burst against the twelve-inch steel.

To the ship itself it did no particular damage. It did not slow the working of the turret; in fact, it left hardly a mark on the diamond-hard steel. Its fragment sang viciously through the air, ripping up planking here and cutting through a stanchion there, but they found no one in an exposed position, and they took no lives. The force of its explosion shook the group on the signal bridge, they felt the hot breath of its flame, and their nostrils were filled with the penetrating stink of its fumes, but they were unhurt. Perhaps of all the hits scored by *Artemis*'s guns this one did the least physical damage, but for all that it was the one which turned the scale. All the other shells fired by *Artemis* had played their part, had leaded the scale so far, had worked upon the minds of Nocentini and von Bödicke, convincing them that here were no easy victims, no weak-minded enemies to be driven off by a mere show of force; but it was this last shell, which Colquhoun had lifted so casually, and which Mobbs and Filmore had sent up to 'A' turret with their minds occupied by Ransome's peevishness, and upon which Sub-Lieutenant Coxe had cast an unseeing eye while Merivale rammed it home, it was this last shell bursting vainly against the turret that actually decided the history of the world.

Nocentini and von Bödicke looked at each other again as they steadied themselves after the explosion. Each was unhurt, each of them hoped breathlessly in his heart of hearts that the other was not. For one second more they hesitated, each hoping that the other would assume the responsibility for the next move, and during that second each of them read the added weakness in the other's face, and they both of them realized that there was no need to state formally what was in their minds. It would be better not to do so, they both decided; it gave each of them more chance to shuffle off the blame – if there was to be blame – upon the other. They did not meet each other's eyes after that; von Bödicke looked at Klein while Nocentini turned to Lorenzetti.

'Signal all ships turn together eight points to starboard,' said Nocentini. He was shoulder to shoulder with von Bödicke, and he did his best to convey by his bearing the impression that the two of them were in complete agreement on the decision, while von Bödicke, the moment he heard the decisive words tried to put himself in an attitude of ineffective protest without attracting Nocentini's attention to it.

The flags ran up to the yardarm, flapped there in the smoke, were answered and were hauled down, Slowly *Legnano* turned her ponderous bulk about, her bows towards Italy, her stern to the British squadron.

'We had to do it,' said Nocentini. 'Otherwise we would have crossed the course of the torpedoes.'

Von Bödicke kept his mouth shut; he only just grasped the meaning of the Italian words, and he was not going to commit himself to anything that might later be construed as approval. He felt much happier in the probability that Nocentini could be saddled with the blame. He walked stiffly to the other end of the bridge, meeting no one's eye as the staffs made way for him, and for Nocentini at his elbow.

From the starboard wing of the bridge he could look down the long line abreast of the Italian fleet. The heavy cruiser on the far side of *San Martino* was still badly on fire. That would be part of his defence, if he should need defence. The guns had fallen silent, for the sudden change of course had disconcerted the trainers, and only half of *Legnano*'s armament could bear on a target right astern. And yet at that very moment another broadside from the British came crashing home as though the ship were suddenly struck by a Titanic sledgehammer. Some fragment hurled by the explosion rang loudly against the stanchion at his side. It was the last straw to von Bödicke that the British should persist in continuing the fight when he had allowed it to be broken off on the Italian side. He wanted to relax, to allow the tension to lessen, and yet the British were set upon continuing the action to the last possible moment.

Legnano's upper works aft were riven into picturesque ruin, he saw. No vital damage done, but enough to make a deep impression on any civilian who might see it. That was all to the good. But Klein knew better. Klein, who had crossed the bridge and was standing at his elbow again, and whom he suspected strongly of being a spy on behalf of Fricke. Von Bödicke hated Klein.

'They are holding their course,' said Nocentini from behind his binoculars, which were trained on the British cruisers. He was speaking careful French, and von Bödicke realized that although the words were apparently addressed to him, Nocentini meant them to be recorded by Klein. 'They will not leave their smoke screen.'

'That is clear,' said von Bödicke, agreeing speedily. He hoped as he spoke them Klein would not perceive the stilted artificiality of his tone; it was ingenious of Nocentini to suggest that the turn-away was really planned to lure the British cruisers away from their smoke screen.

'We will re-form line ahead when the torpedoes have passed,' said Nocentini.

'Of course,' said von Bödicke. He had himself under control now. He kept his eyes steadily on the Italian and did now allow them to waver towards Klein for a moment. It was undignified and sordid, but defeat is always undignified and sordid. They were beaten men.

They were already out of range of the British cruisers, and the distance was increasing every minute. When they should form line ahead again and circle round to reopen the engagement it would be nearly dark, and no sane officer would court a night action with an inferior force. Someone was yelling madly from the masthead, his high-pitched voice clearly audible from the signal bridge, although von Bödicke could not understand the excited Italian. *Legnano* swung ponderously round again, under full helm, first to port and then to starboard – it was that, combined with the rush of the Italian officers to the side, and the way they peered down at the water, which told von Bödicke that the track of a torpedo had been sighted, and that *Legnano* was manoeuvring to avoid it. He caught his breath quickly. The gestures of the Italians showed that the torpedo had passed, and then directly afterwards there came the roar of an explosion to split the eardrums. The torpedo which *Legnano* had avoided had struck *San Martino* full in the side. An enormous column of water, higher than the funnel top, obscured the battleship momentarily before it cascaded back into the sea and revealed her with smoke pouring out of her side and listing perceptibly.

He caught Nocentini's eye again as the Admiral stood rapping out orders. The anxiety and strain had gone from the man's face. He was dealing with a familiar emergency, one with which he was competent to deal. Salving and protecting an injured ship was not like carrying the burden of the responsibility of battle. And not only that, but the problems of battle were solved for him. No one could expect him to leave an injured Dreadnought to shift for herself while he turned and re-engaged the enemy. No one could expect him to. A Nelson or a Beatty might take the risk, but no man could be condemned for not being a Nelson or Beatty. Nocentini actually smiled a little as he met von Bödicke's eye, and von Bödicke smiled back. Whatever happened now, they had at least an explanation and an excuse.

26

From the Captain's Report
. . . and the action terminated.

The Captain had known temptation. With *Artemis* all ablaze aft, and one turret out of action, it was a strain to keep her in action, dodging the continual salvoes of the enemy. The very din of the continual broadsides was exhausting. Close at hand, on the port side, was the shelter of the smoke screen. He had only to utter two words and *Artemis* could dive into it just as she had done before. There would be a relief from strain and danger and responsibility, and the thought even of relief that might be only momentary was alluring. And the whole principle of the tactics of the British cruisers was to make use of the smoke screen as it rolled down on the Italian line; now that the destroyers had delivered their attack and turned back would be a fitting moment, ostensibly, for a temporary withdrawal. That was the temptation on the one hand, while on the other was the doubt of his own judgement that it was desirable to continue in action. That might be just fighting madness. He knew that his judgement might be clouded, that this decision of his to keep his guns firing might be the result of mere berserk rage. Yet his instinct told him that it was not so.

His instinct; something developed in him by years of study of his profession, of deep reading and of mental digestion of innumerable lessons, supplemented by his inborn qualities. That instinct told him that this was the crisis of the battle, the moment when one side or the other must give way. He knew that he had only to hold on a little longer – after that a little longer still, perhaps – for the battle to be decided. The whole series of thoughts, from the decision to cover the retreat of the destroyers to the momentary doubt, and then back again to the decision to maintain the action took only the briefest possible time, two or three seconds at most.

It was not to the discredit of the Captain that he should have experienced that two or three seconds of doubt, but to his credit. Had he not been tried so far as that it would have been no trial at all. War is something to try the very strongest, and it is then that those crack who are almost the strongest, the Nocentinis and the von Bödickes, oppressed by a complexity of motives.

The Captain was aware that his pipe was empty, and that he wanted to refill and relight it, but he did not want to take his binoculars from his eyes. The guns of 'A' and 'B' turrets roared out below him; the Captain did not know that from the left-hand gun of 'A' turret had flown the decisive shell. He saw the flight of the broadside, and he saw the yellow flash of the hit. Then, as another broadside roared out disregarded, he saw the long silhouette of the leading Italian battleship foreshorten and alter, the two funnels blend into one, the stern swinging towards him and the bow away. The Captain gulped excitedly. He traversed his binoculars round. Every Italian ship had her stern to him; it was a withdrawal, a retreat; the Italian flagship was not merely trying to disconnect the English gunners. This was victory.

He turned his gaze back to the Italian flagship in time to see the flash of another hit upon her. Good gunnery, that, to hit at that extreme range and with the range altering so fast. He dropped his glasses on his chest and took out pipe and pouch, feeding tobacco into the bowl with his long sensitive fingers, but his eyes still strained after the distant shapes on the horizon. They had turned away. They were refusing battle. The Captain knew in his bones that they would never turn back again to re-open the fight. A motive strong enough to induce them to break off the fight would be amply strong enough to keep them from renewing it; one way or the other they would find excuses for themselves.

His pipe was filled, and he was just reaching for his matches when the voice pipe buzzer sounded:

'Director Control,' said the pipe. 'The enemy is out of range.'

'Thank you, Guns,' said the Captain. 'I have no orders for you at present.'

The Chief Yeoman of Signals saluted.

'I think I saw a torpedo 'it on the second ship from the left,' he said, 'while you was speaking.'

'Thank you,' said the Captain again.

He was about to take up his binoculars to look, but he changed his mind and felt for his matches instead. He could afford to be prodigal of his time and his attention now. Even a torpedo hit on a Dreadnought was nothing in the scale compared with the fact of the Italian turn away. The tobacco tasted good as he drew the flame of the match down upon it, stoppered it down with the finger that long use had rendered comparatively fireproof, and drew on the flame again. He breathed out a lungful of smoke and carefully dropped the stump of the match into the spit-kid. The silence and the cessation of the enemy's fire were ceasing to be oppressive; the normal sounds of the ship's progress, the noise of the sea under the bows and of the wind about his ears, were asserting themselves.

So this was victory. The proof that the history of the world had reached a turning point was that he was conscious again of the wind about his ears. History books would never write about today. Even sober, scientific historians needed some more solid fact on which to hang a theme; a few ships sunk and a few thousand men killed, not a mere successful skirmish round half a dozen transports. Even in a month's time the memory of today would be faded and forgotten by the world. Two lines in a communiqué, a few remarks by appreciative commentators, and then oblivion.

Somewhere out in the Russian plain Ivan Ivanovich, crouching in a hole in the dusty earth, and looking along the sights of his anti-tank gun, would never know about *Artemis* and her sisters. Ivan Ivanovich might comment on the slightness of the aerial attack, on the scarcity of hostile dive bombers; it might even occur to him as a realist that a few well-placed bombs, wiping out him and his fellows, could clear the way into Moscow for Hitler, but even as a realist Ivan Ivanovich had never heard of *Artemis*, and never would hear.

To Hitler, Malta was a prize still more desirable than Moscow, and more vital to his existence. With the failure of the Italian navy to get it for him he would have to use his own air force; a thousand planes, and a ground staff scores of thousands strong would have to be transferred from the Russian front to Italy in the desperate need to conquer every bastion that could buttress his top-heavy empire. A thousand planes; planes that could blind the Russian command, planes that could blast a path through the Russian lines, planes that could succour isolated detachments and supply advance guards, planes that could hunt Russian guerrilla forces far in the rear of the Germans or menace Russian communications far in advance. The Captain had no doubt whatever that as a result of today's work those thousand planes would be brought south.

Whether they would achieve their object or not was more doubtful. The Captain had the feeling that the advocates of air power talked about today as if it were tomorrow. Tomorrow command of the air might take the place of command of the sea, but this was today. Today those half-dozen fat transports wallowing along on the far side of the smoke screen were on their way to Malta, and it was today they had to be stopped, if at all. Today the convoys were still pouring in to English harbours, while across a tiny strip of water lay an enemy whose greatest ambition was to prevent them from doing so. It was sea power that brought them safely in. Tomorrow it might be air power; tomorrow the Captain might be an antiquated old fogey, as useless as a pikeman on a modern battlefield, but the war was being fought today, today, today. Rommel in Libya clamouring for reinforcement could have everything his heart desired if the British Navy did not interfere. The crippling of the American Navy at Pearl Harbour had put an eighth of the world's population and a quarter of the world's surface temporarily at the mercy of Japan and her twelve Dreadnoughts. Ships – ships and the men in them – were still deciding the fate of the world. The Arab fertilizing date palms at Basra, the Negro trading cattle for a new wife in Central Africa, the gaucho riding the Argentine pampas, did so under the protection of the British Navy, of which the Captain and his ship were a minor fraction, one of many parts whose sum was equal to the whole.

'Signal from the flagship, sir,' said the Chief Yeoman of Signals, reading it off through his glass: 'Resume – convoy – formation.'

'Acknowledge,' said the Captain.

He gave the order to turn *Artemis* back towards the transports, back through the smoke screen which had served them so well. The revolution indicator rang down a reduction of speed, and peace seemed to settle closer about the ship as the vibration caused by full speed died away. Only a tiny bit of the sun was left, a segment of gold on the clear horizon – ten seconds more and it would be gone and night would close in. The Italians were already invisible from the bridge, and the Captain strode abruptly over to the masthead voice pipe.

'Masthead,' said the tube to him in answer to his buzz. It was Ordinary Seaman Whipple's voice.

'Can you see anything of the enemy?' asked the Captain.

'Only just in sight, sir. They're still heading away from us. They'll be gone in a minute.'

They were close clipped, incisive sentences which Whipple used. Whipple was conscious of victory, too. He was fighting for an ideal, and he was fanatical about that ideal, and this afternoon's work had brought that ideal a great deal closer. Yet Whipple did not indulge in idle exhilaration. The fact that he had to fight for his ideal, that the generation preceding his had once had the same ideal in their grasp and allowed it to slip through their fingers, had left him without illusions. Whipple was ready to go on fighting. He knew there was still a long bitter struggle ahead before final victory, and he guessed that after victory it would be another bitter struggle to put it to the best use, to forward the ideal, and he was ready for both struggles.

The Captain in his present clairvoyant mood could sense all this in the tone of Whipple's voice, and he drew once, meditatively, on his pipe before he turned away. One part of his mind was concerned in practical fashion with the future promotion of Whipple to leading Seaman; the other was thinking how Whipple's generation, twenty years younger than his own, must take up the task of building the good of the new world as unfalteringly as they were applying themselves to the task of tearing down the evil of the old world, in each case facing random defeat, and unexpected disappointment, and peril and self-sacrifice, with selfless self-discipline.

As he looked up from the voice pipe his eyes met those of his secretary.

'Congratulations, sir,' said Jerningham.

So Jerningham was aware of the importance of today, too. The rest of the ship's company, going quietly about their duties, had not yet attained to that realization. But it was to be expected of Jerningham. His civilian background, the breadth of his experience and the liveliness of his imagination, made him able – when he was not too closely concerned personally – to take a wide view of the war, and to realize how proper attention to his own duties would help Ivan Ivanovich in his hole in the ground, or Lai Chao tearing up a railway line in Shantung. There was a moment of sympathy between Jerningham and the Captain, during which brief space of time they were *en rapport*, each appreciative of the other.

'Thank you, Jerningham,' said the Captain.

This was no time to relax, to indulge either in futile congratulations or in idle speculation. The smoke screen suddenly engulfed the ship; it was not nearly as dense as when it had first been laid, but with the rapid approach of night now that the sun was below the horizon the darkness inside the smoke screen was intense. The Captain took three strides in the darkness to the end of the bridge and craned his neck to look aft. There was only the faintest glow to be seen of the fire which had raged there, and a few more minutes with the hoses would extinguish even that.

They emerged into the evening light again; the scant minute during which they had been in the smoke screen seemed to have brought night far closer. There was just light enough to see how the fires and the enemy's hits had left the whole after third of the ship above water line a tangle of burnt-out steel, a nightmare of buckled plates and twisted girders, desolate and dead.

Artemis under the orders of the Navigating Lieutenant

was wheeling round to take the station allotted her by the standing orders for convoy escort at night. It was as well that the fires had been subdued, for otherwise the flames would be a welcoming beacon inviting a torpedo. The aeroplanes had attacked in the morning; in the afternoon they had beaten off the surface ships; tonight they would have to be on their guard against submarines, for the enemy, like the devil, was capable of taking many forms. One battle completed, one victory achieved, merely meant that *Artemis* and her men must plunge headlong into the next, into the long struggle of sea power against tyranny; the struggle that the Greeks had waged at Salamis, that the Captain's ancestors had waged against the Armada of Spain, against the fleets of Louis XIV and Napoleon and Wilhelm II, the long struggle which some day would have an end, but not now, and not for months and years to come. And even when it should end the freedom which the struggle would win could only be secured by eternal vigilance, eternal probity, eternal good will, and eternal honesty of purpose. That would be the hardest lesson of it; peace would be a severer test of mankind even than war. Perhaps mankind would pass that test when the time came; and when that time came (the Captain said to himself) he would fight to the last, he would die in the last ditch, before he would compromise in the slightest with the blind or secret enemies of freedom and justice. He must remember this mood; when he became an old man he must remember it. He must remember in time to come how nothing now was farther from his thoughts than the least yielding to the open enemies of mankind, and that would help to keep him from the least indolent or careless or cynical yielding in that future.

The Captain suddenly tensed himself as his roving eyes caught sight of a twinkle of light ahead, and then he was able to relax again and even smile a little to himself in the twilight. For that was the evening star shining out over the Mediterranean.